Lucy didn't resist him

Guy reached for her slowly, giving her plenty of time to resist—but she didn't. The embrace was inevitable.

Her eyes closed as his hand slid beneath her hair to close warmly around her nape. Feeling flooded through her, a soft velvet warmth raced from the core of her being.

"I can't help it."

She thought the words were in her mind only, but Guy's head lifted just as his lips began to close over hers. His eyes burned with something that wasn't scorn—it was a flare of excitement. His face darkened and he drew her completely into his arms.

"Why try to?" he murmured. "Our fate was decided the moment I saw you."

PATRICIA WILSON used to live in Yorkshire, England, but with her children all grown-up, she decided to give up her teaching position there and accompany her husband on an extended trip to Spain. Their travels are providing her with plenty of inspiration for her romance writing.

Books by Patricia Wilson

HARLEQUIN PRESENTS

1221—THE GATHERING DARKNESS
1238—TEMPORARY BRIDE
1262—GUARDIAN ANGEL
1286—DANGEROUS OBSESSION
1310—A SECRET UNDERSTANDING
1398—PASSIONATE ENEMY
1430—STORMY SURRENDER
1454—CURTAIN OF STARS

HARLEQUIN ROMANCE

2856—BRIDE OF DIAZ
3102—BOND OF DESTINY

Don't miss any of our special offers. Write to us at the following address for information on our newest releases.

Harlequin Reader Service
P.O. Box 1397, Buffalo, NY 14240
Canadian address: P.O. Box 603,
Fort Erie, Ont. L2A 5X3

PATRICIA WILSON

the gift of loving

Harlequin Books

TORONTO • NEW YORK • LONDON
AMSTERDAM • PARIS • SYDNEY • HAMBURG
STOCKHOLM • ATHENS • TOKYO • MILAN
MADRID • WARSAW • BUDAPEST • AUCKLAND

Harlequin Presents first edition June 1992
ISBN 0-373-11469-9

Original hardcover edition published in 1991
by Mills & Boon Limited

THE GIFT OF LOVING

CHAPTER ONE

'HE's here, just as I predicted!' Wanda Balfour grasped Lucy's arm eagerly, her voice low but triumphant. 'Your first glimpse of a count, Lucinda. Get a good look at him. You'll be seeing a lot of him soon.'

Lucy looked across the foyer at the man who had just come into the hotel, her face amused at her aunt's enthusiasm. Her heart sank like a stone at the sight of him. He looked coldly autocratic, exactly her idea of how a French aristocrat would look, and she hoped she would be seeing nothing of him at all, because he wasn't what she had expected. He wasn't old for a start.

Tall and dark, his face composed, and just a trifle bored, he was coldly handsome. He looked utterly unapproachable and how her aunt expected to attract his attention Lucy didn't know, in fact she was sure it would be impossible. For the first time ever she had doubts about working for Wanda.

'Ah! *Monsieur le Comte*. Your suite is ready of course. Your luggage has arrived.'

The receptionist snapped to self-important attention but the count merely nodded, collecting his key and turning away. He moved as effortlessly and as powerfully as an athlete, his dark eyes scanning the foyer with very little interest, and Lucy still watched in fascination. It was a commanding face, calm, still, expressionless like the painting of some god who didn't quite see mortals.

He looked across, the dark eyes meeting hers unexpectedly, and shock hit her deep inside, alarm bells ringing wildly. His eyes were brilliantly alive, sparkling like sunlight off jet, the same command in them that

was in his face. The glittering glance swept over her, his
black brows rising in aloof surprise, and she looked
hastily away, fixing her eyes on the carpet, her face
flooding with colour.

Her heart was racing. At this rate she was going to
upset all her aunt's plans. She only relaxed when she
heard the sound of the lift doors closing and the quiet
hum that announced its departure. One glance had
unsettled her easygoing nature and her skin felt shivery.

'He looked across at us, anyway. He noticed us at
once,' Wanda Balfour said with an air of total satisfaction, glee edging her voice. 'It's a very good
beginning.'

'He didn't look across at us pleasantly, Aunt Wanda,'
Lucy pointed out quickly, astonished that her aunt had
not seen the danger in that face. She could very well do
without him looking at her again at any time. She felt
as if something powerful had brushed against her. It was
almost like having a narrow escape. 'He seemed to be
quite annoyed.'

'Of course he wasn't, Lucinda! You don't understand
these people. You have to realise that they're not like
anyone else. Take the count for example. His ancestors
were nobility in France in the days of Joan of Arc. By
the time of the revolution they were one of the most
powerful families in the country. Their history will be
fascinating!'

'Are you sure he'll want to——?' Lucy began hopefully, but her aunt silenced her with a wave of the hand.

'He'll be delighted to have his family in one of my
books. They always are delighted. As soon as he knows
who I am he'll change. You'll see.'

Lucy lapsed into an embarrassed, guilty silence. She
had read one of her aunt's books and had been astonished that it had ever been published. Maybe her aunt
had enthused at the publisher as she enthused at everyone
else? Wanda Balfour was utterly engrossed by the idea

of nobility, especially French nobility, and she had
written several books on the descendants of the families
who had survived the French Revolution, providing that
they still had their châteaux and land intact. Aunt Wanda
loved staying with them and gloating over their treasures
as if they were her own. Lucy supposed it was some sort
of obsession.

She also felt guilty about her private thoughts. Coming
to France with her aunt was a real thrill, the chance of
a lifetime. Now that she had seen her aunt's next subject,
though, the thrill was edged with deep unease, almost
fear, as if she were on the verge of some abyss.

'I'll give him a day and then we'll approach him,'
Wanda said comfortably, getting ready to move.

'*We?* I... I can't... You don't expect me...? I wouldn't
know what to say! I...'

'Don't act like a frightened mouse!' Her aunt's amused
glance moved over her. 'You even look like a frightened
mouse. You're not in that dingy office now and you're
not at your mother's beck and call. You're working for
me and we move in style!'

Wanda Balfour stood and made her way to the door,
leaving Lucy with no alternative but to follow, although
the busy, colourful streets of Paris gave her less
enjoyment than they had done earlier. They were certainly moving in style, staying at the hotel that housed
the Comte de Chauvrais! It must be costing her aunt a
small fortune.

Lucy's creamy brow furrowed as she hurried after
Wanda. Maybe the books did better than she had
imagined? Her aunt didn't seem to have a care in the
world. It was that bright self-assurance that had finally
made Lucy decide to give up her safe little job and agree
to work for Wanda as companion and secretary. It had
seemed like a huge step into the future, a chance to live
at last.

She had given that same job up twice actually, once to look after her mother for three painful years and now again to go with her aunt. After her mother had died there had been a vacancy again at her old place of work, a small estate agent's office in the country town she had lived close to all her life. There was no money in her family and even the life assurance premiums had not been paid. The manager had been sympathetic, taking her back into her old job, and he had not been best pleased when she left again after such a short time. It had been a chance to really live though, coming with her aunt. It had seemed glamorous. In fact it had seemed glamorous until she had seen the count. Now she wasn't at all sure.

She caught a glimpse of herself in a shop window and grimaced. She looked uninteresting, almost drab. She was twenty-three, her figure too slim, her legs too slender. Her hair was long and straight, not quite brown and not quite blonde—nondescript! Her face was a perfect oval but too pale now after the years of hard work and anxiety over her mother, making her dark blue eyes look over-large in her face.

Mouse! It was a good description. Even her brown suit enhanced that appearance. The skirt was too short and she felt very self-conscious, not that anyone spared her more than a glance. She would have liked to buy a longer skirt, one that covered more of her legs. Aunt Wanda was doing everything else for her, though, and there would be no pay for this work until the whole project was finished. She was to get her keep and nothing more until then. It was what she had agreed to with some eagerness and she couldn't very well ask for money for clothes now.

She knew her aunt didn't really need a companion. It was true that Lucy could type well, but she had no certificates to prove it. Wanda was just being kind, giving her a chance to see something of life. She hurried after her aunt and smiled brightly. Until today she had been thrilled. She was not about to let an arrogant-looking Frenchman unsettle her. Her aunt's amused glance told her that Wanda had noted that she had 'come to her senses' and she squashed all rebellion and fear. Aunt Wanda had rescued her from a drab existence. What was she worrying about?

Her aunt intrigued her, and how she knew where her latest subject would be at any given time was a mystery that Lucy had not solved.

'It's worth the expenditure,' Wanda had confided comfortably. 'After all, I have very little outlay for my work. Once my subject is interested I move in with them to have the use of their library and so on, and after that it's just the cost of the paper.'

It was a wonderfully blithe way of going about things and Lucy hoped she was going to earn her keep. She had spent too many years looking after other people to have had any time for real training.

'Let's get you a new dress for dinner tonight,' Wanda said in her usual determined manner, firmly squashing Lucy's anxious protests. 'You've got to look the part, my dear.'

What part? Maybe it was simply not to disgrace Wanda with her very ordinary clothes? Her aunt dressed expensively, though a trifle colourfully. Lucy submitted and when they went back to the hotel she had a straight blue dress that picked up the colour of her eyes. It was not at all glamorous but it was the most expensive dress she had ever possessed.

At dinner, the count was not there, much to Wanda's annoyance and Lucy's great relief. At the back of her mind she could still see the aloof displeasure on his face when he had caught her looking at him. She had known all about how her aunt worked but she had envisaged some old man, some elderly aristocrat engrossed in his books and as enthusiastic as her aunt, someone who would look at her with vague and kindly eyes. The Comte de Chauvrais had eyes that glittered like black ice. Kindness looked very alien to him. She sincerely hoped that this time her aunt's plans would come unstuck. There were other aristocrats with other books.

Next morning Lucy went along to her aunt's room before breakfast, determined to do any jobs that presented themselves. If she didn't begin to work in a sort of professional manner then her conscience was going to get the better of her. This was not a holiday. She was supposed to be assisting her aunt. Instead she was busy wishing disaster on well-laid plans.

'Go down and see if there's any mail for me at Reception, Lucinda,' her aunt asked as soon as she saw her.

Wanda was not ready to eat and Lucy went down in the lift feeling a little more light-hearted, a good night's sleep having vanquished dark, glittering eyes. There were several letters and Lucy decided to walk back up the two flights of stairs; it would delay her arrival and mean she was not simply hanging around waiting as her aunt was nowhere near ready.

At the top of the last flight she swung round the corner a little too briskly, bumping headlong into a man who was just coming in the opposite direction. Her impetus almost knocked her off balance and the letters flew from her hand as she staggered.

Strong hands steadied her, holding her fast, and she found herself looking up into the dark eyes of the man who had quite scared her yesterday, as the Comte de Chauvrais held her shoulders and looked down at her with the same aloof surprise he had shown before.

'Oh! I—I'm sorry...'

'*Ça ne fait rien, mademoiselle,*' he murmured coolly, looking as if it mattered a great deal, and Lucy went on staring up at him until the black eyebrows rose yet again and her face flushed painfully.

'Th-thank you,' she managed breathlessly, as he relaxed his hold. He scooped up the letters before she had the chance to move and handed them to her courteously but her blushes deepened as he stared into her eyes.

'Thank you.' There wasn't a lot more she could say, and close up he was having a very alarming influence on her. He had almost robbed her of the ability to speak, for one thing. She was aware of the leashed-in power of the body so close to her as if danger was all around her.

'My pleasure, *mademoiselle*.' The sardonic voice dropped easily into English. 'Perhaps in future I will take the lift. Stairs appear to present a certain amount of hazard.'

Lucy was glad he couldn't see her as he went down the stairs. She was still embarrassed and strangely breathless, but his sardonic tone was so much at one with his appearance that she felt a wave of unaccustomed annoyance.

She had long ago learned to keep control of what was a quite fiery temper. It had been utterly useless with the vague ways of her parents, but this man was irritating, all the more so when she knew it would not be long before her aunt pounced on him and caused even further embarrassment. He would simply look at them coldly and walk away. She found that she was leaning against the wall, her hand to her throat. She had to shake her head to fully recover.

Wanda was ready, well made-up and slightly exotic-looking in a flowered dress, by the time Lucy got back to the bedroom and they went down to have breakfast. Lucy was in one of her skirts and a very plain sweater, at least looking the part of companion and secretary. If she kept on looking like that then this affair would have very little to do with her; he would stare into her aunt's eyes instead. The thought gave her a great deal of comfort and she composed her face accordingly, carefully walking just one step behind her aunt.

He was in the dining-room! Lucy saw him immediately and her heart sank as Wanda walked right over towards him, only turning at the last minute to go to their own table, deliberately seeking his attention.

He looked up and Wanda beamed at him graciously.

'Bonjour, monsieur,' she murmured, and it obviously took him by surprise but he half rose and bowed slightly.

'Madame.' He did not extend the greeting to Lucy but his eyes slid over her sceptically before his glance flashed to hers. It was only for a second but she felt flustered as if he had taken an instant inventory of her clothes and appearance. They did not interest him at all. He ignored everyone and continued to eat, and as her aunt had manoeuvred them so close it was not possible for her to congratulate herself aloud. She did that as the count left the dining-room.

'Stage two completed,' she announced smugly. 'Perhaps tonight at dinner...'

Lucy hoped not. She spent the rest of the day just thinking about it and almost drowning in imagined embarrassment. Her aunt must be quite mad, after all. It was very obvious that the count would know at once what she was after. Those dark, ironic eyes were rather frighteningly intelligent. That quick glance had been probing and alert. She shuddered when she wondered what he would say.

He seemed to be playing right into Wanda's hands, though, because when dinnertime came and Lucy was once more in the straight blue dress, walking into the very opulent cocktail bar with her aunt, the count was there already, right by the door, just waiting to be captured, and Wanda was not slow to act.

'Bonsoir, monsieur.' This time the rather sardonic face relaxed into a sort of half-smile.

'Good evening, *madame*. We appear to have met again.'

Lucy looked at him closely from beneath her lashes but his face gave no clue to his state of mind and her aunt pounced rapidly.

'You speak English? How very nice. I *do* speak French but it's most kind of you to reply in my own language, though how you knew...'

'It is a certain something in the accent, *madame*. In any case, I take every opportunity to practise my English. I would be grateful for the chance to practise it now. You will allow me to buy you a drink?'

Wanda most certainly would, and the dark eyes then turned on Lucy.

'*Mademoiselle?*'

She just stared at him, utterly tongue-tied, quite out of her league. She saw a glitter of amusement start in the dark eyes and Wanda interrupted this rather dazed interlude briskly.

'My niece will take a small sherry, *monsieur*. This is her first time abroad.'

One black eyebrow rose slightly, although he nodded pleasantly enough, but as he turned away to give his order, Lucy didn't miss the slight, disdainful smile that edged his lips. She wondered if the ground ever did open up and swallow people? She wished it would perform that service for her now.

He couldn't have been as intelligent as he looked because he invited them to his table for dinner and talked quite easily with her aunt. If Wanda noticed that his eyes frequently strayed rather disparagingly to her niece then she never commented. She was too busy talking to bring Lucy into the conversation and Lucy was heartily glad of it. She felt like a servant who had been asked to dine with nobility. She spent so much time avoiding the dark eyes that flashed constantly to hers that she hardly tasted anything.

She heard when her aunt began to reel off her literary achievements though, quoting widely from her anecdotes of the French aristocracy pre-revolution, and Lucy could hardly believe her ears when he walked right into that too.

'My own family is not without history, *madame*,' he informed her quietly. 'We are one of the oldest noble families in France.'

'I most certainly beg your pardon.' Wanda's face was delightfully confused, a masterpiece of acting. 'I've been so busy talking about myself, *monsieur*, that I never even thought of making a correct introduction. I'm Wanda Balfour and this is my niece Lucinda.'

'Guy Chabrol, *madame*, Comte de Chauvrais, although it is a title I rarely use. It is now quite worthless.'

'Oh, surely not, *monsieur*! It's one of the most famous names in France. Your past must be absolutely bursting with fascinating history.'

Having walked right into it, he kept on coming.

'If it interests you, *madame*, I would be honoured to allow you to search my family records. I have a large and fascinating library in my château. Many of the books have not been touched since my grandfather's time. You are welcome to use them.'

'You're so *kind*!' Wanda gushed, her enthusiasm like a tidal wave. 'Is the château close to Paris?'

'No. I'm afraid not. It is bordering on the Loire.'

'Oh. How disappointing. It would be an impossibility to travel there from here and really work.' Wanda's face was a picture of disappointment and Lucy was stunned into reluctant admiration at the way her aunt had let this arrogant Frenchman walk into the trap. What really puzzled her was that he had just waded right in there.

'But of course you would be invited to stay with me, *madame*,' he said, evidently surprised that she should think otherwise. 'Perhaps if you are sufficiently interested you would also write about my family? It would be very nice to have our history well documented for future generations.'

'Perhaps, *monsieur*, your wife would not...?'

'I do not have a wife, *madame*. My stepmother lives at the château and there are of course the servants. Your niece is also invited,' he added with a dark, sidelong look at Lucy that told her she was part of her aunt's baggage and therefore not to be lost en route. Her face flared with colour and the long lips quirked in amusement but Wanda was delighted and talked even more. It was only later as they moved to the coffee lounge and her aunt went to powder her nose that Lucy found herself left alone with Guy Chabrol, trapped by dark eyes that looked at her intently.

'And what do *you* do, *mademoiselle*, in this whirl of literary energy?'

'I—I've come with my aunt as secretary and companion.' Lucy felt her face flushing and his raised eyebrows did nothing to help.

'So you do speak your own language after all?' he murmured ironically. 'I was beginning to wonder if you only knew how to say "sorry" and "thank you". I would have imagined that a secretary and companion needed to have some modicum of conversation.'

The disdain was back with some force and Lucy felt a wave of annoyance that drowned out her shyness.

'This is my first job with Aunt Wanda,' she said crossly. 'When I meet someone I like I'll have no difficulty at all in speaking.'

Her sharp reply merely astonished him further and he chose to overlook the insolence.

'What did you do before this excursion?' he asked briefly, his tone so commanding that Lucy replied without thought.

'I lived with my mother and father. I helped them and then I——'

She didn't have the chance to tell him about her job. He cut in ruthlessly.

'So, you are a helper?' he enquired drily, one dark brow raised sarcastically. 'Anything from Cinderella to a bookkeeper. I now understand your silence. You are a professional shadow. Perhaps you will be able to help me?'

'I only help my family,' Lucy said tightly, her face more flushed than ever at his taunting, but she had only given him further ammunition.

'Ah! I see. You are a poor relation, *n'est-ce pas*?'

Lucy felt explosive. He was the rudest and most arrogant man she had ever met. She saw her aunt coming purposefully back, her eyes alert at Lucy's expression. Naturally, Wanda didn't want the boat rocked now and she fixed her eye on Lucy.

'Yes, *monsieur*,' Lucy said, standing and looking down at him. 'I'm a very poor relation. You'll find that out soon enough if we stay with you. Don't worry, though, I don't eat much and I can always sleep on the floor!'

He stood as Wanda came back but his eyes were intently on Lucy, the glitter of laughter deep in their dark depths.

'I should get off to bed, if I were you, Lucinda,' her aunt said quickly. 'You look tired.'

'I have perhaps wearied her with my conversation,' Guy Chabrol murmured, his dark face sardonic. 'Goodnight, *mademoiselle*.'

His eyes were probing again, watchful and questioning, and Lucy fled without a word. He was much worse than he had appeared to be on first sight. He wasn't coldly aristocratic, he was cruel. He had probed her weakness and left her feeling worthless. To her astonishment she felt tears in her eyes and she couldn't get to her room fast enough.

A poor relation! She hadn't felt like one until now, but she supposed she was, in any case. She got ready for bed and then lay in the darkness, her mind taking a critical look at her past life. There wasn't a lot of it, she decided ruefully. Her early role in life had been to admire somebody. First her parents and now Aunt Wanda. They had all been the same type, she realised, part of a small group of artistic people who fed off praise.

None of them had been particularly talented. Her mother had been an artist, not exactly successful but making enough to keep the wolf from the door. Her father had written poetry, almost all of it unsaleable, mostly written for self-satisfaction, his greatest audience the few people who moved in the same circle, his 'set'.

Looking back, Lucy often wondered how they had survived at all. It was only the Old Mill that had kept them going. It was an old building that her mother and father had rented and turned into both a home and a place of work. Her mother had done small pictures to sell, her father had written poems on parchment that tourists bought to hang in their homes. The fact that the things had been originals had not made them good but it had kept a small amount of money coming in. They had survived.

How Lucy had survived as a baby in this odd and disordered household was a mystery, but as she got older she had more or less taken them both under her wing. They had been quite incapable of looking after themselves or paying the bills that came in. Luckily the bills had been few. It had been a spartan existence. She had taken a job in town, a rather dull job in a dull establishment, her additional salary making it possible to give a few luxuries to her parents. She wasn't at all sure if they had even noticed.

Her father had died when she was eighteen. Lucy had been a child of their later years, and two years after that, with her mother elderly and ailing, Lucy had relin-

quished her job and her small amount of independence,
her odd night out, and moved back to her earlier role,
taking care of someone, bowing to their peculiarities.

Maybe that was why she had taken the risk of coming
out here with her aunt? Right now, though, Lucy would
have given anything to be back at the Old Mill, walking
barefoot to the river through fields bright with buttercups, the soft green grass sweet-smelling beneath her feet.

She tossed restlessly, her mind leaving the past, and
instantly dark, scathing eyes came into her mind, cold
with disdain. She had never before met anyone who had
got so thoroughly under her skin. She had a patient,
understanding nature but Guy Chabrol had stabbed at
her self-esteem, probing her inner lack of confidence like
a hot steel wire. She would have to face him anyway.
She resolutely tried to sleep. She had faced worse.

Apparently many arrangements had been made the night
before, because when Lucy presented herself at her aunt's
room the next day she was informed that they would be
leaving immediately after breakfast.

'Are—are we going to this château?'

'Of course we are, Lucinda.' Wanda looked at her as
if she were mad. 'I've put a lot of work into this project,
not to speak of the expense. We can live free of charge
at the château for as long as it takes.'

'How long will it take?' Lucy asked with a certain
amount of misery, and received a very odd look from
her aunt.

'That—depends,' she murmured, a very strange smile
on her face. 'Meanwhile, we certainly won't starve. The
count is a financier, absolutely rolling in money. The
château is huge. Stop worrying, my dear. He'll never
even notice us once we're there.'

Lucy wanted to say 'Don't you believe it' but she kept
quiet. That man noticed just about everything. She went

to breakfast with great misgivings, thankful that he wasn't there.

When they came down with their luggage, though, he was right there at the reception desk, turning with a smile to her aunt.

'I have taken care of your account, *madame*. If you are ready we will now leave. It is quite a long way to the château.'

'Oh, but really! I can't allow you to pay my bill,' Wanda protested. He waved her protest aside.

'Have I not commissioned a history of my family, *madame*? This being the case, surely I am now your patron? Naturally I will pay all your expenses.'

Lucy didn't miss the triumph in her aunt's eyes and she was astonished that the count didn't see it too. He looked superbly intelligent and, in any case, he was a financier. He couldn't be that if his head was in the clouds.

For the very first time she looked at him deeply—with suspicion, almost jumping visibly when she found him giving her exactly the same sort of look, the dark eyes narrowed and intent, ignoring her aunt completely, searching and probing into Lucy's mind. She was almost trembling when he turned away and ushered them out to his car, announcing that they would travel with him.

'Make yourself comfortable, *madame*,' he suggested smoothly, helping Wanda into the back of a large black Mercedes. 'Your niece will sit in front with me.'

Lucy's suspicions grew but it was only as they were in the fast-moving traffic, the hotel left behind, that she glanced at him. Her eyes got no further than the brown, capable hands on the wheel. They were long-fingered, graceful, powerful. They looked a little cruel, if hands could look cruel. She just stared at them, her mind going over events.

'Relax, Mademoiselle Balfour,' the dark voice suggested. 'There is quite a way to go but I will have you safely in the château long before nightfall.'

Lucy's hands clenched in her lap. She didn't know what he was up to but she knew there was something. This was not the sort of man who walked blindly into any sort of trap. She had the horrifying feeling that the boot was on the other foot, that *they* had walked into a trap.

He glanced down at her hands, her fingers almost white with the tight clenching, and then his dark eyes flashed to her face.

'You are perfectly safe, *mademoiselle*,' he assured her in a low voice. 'I am not about to stop at the first forest we come to and attack you. In the Château de Rochaine there are servants to guard you. There is my stepmother and, of course, your aunt. I cannot see why you should be so troubled.'

'I'm not,' Lucy said gamely in an equally low voice, thankful that her aunt seemed unable to hear this odd conversation.

'Then relax and enjoy the drive, *mademoiselle*,' he murmured softly. *'Tout va bien.'* His eyes held hers for a second as she looked across at him worriedly and she saw an expression flash deep in his dark gaze that did nothing to reassure her. It was an indefinable spark of something but it was coldly amused, triumphant and, once again, cruel.

CHAPTER TWO

'NOT too far now,' Guy Chabrol announced as they sped past Orleans. He had not addressed one single word to Lucy after his assurance that everything was all right. They had come at great speed down the motorway from Paris but he was so very capable, his hands so skilled on the wheel, that she had to admit she had not once felt any quirk of alarm in that direction.

Her alarmed suspicions had gradually left her and even the fact that they were almost there did nothing to upset her now. She felt a great deal more safe when he kept silent and this was merely an announcement.

They were heading into the valley of the River Loire, and she looked around with interest that was mixed with wonder as she saw the châteaux that were visible along their route. Some were quite small, merely country houses, but most of them were towering and grand. Many of the châteaux were close to pretty villages and somehow the whole idea looked a good deal safer.

They had left the motorway some time back and as he turned from the main road the car began to cross much wilder land. The countryside was now almost deserted as they drove past winding tributaries and small lakes. It was thickly wooded here, much more sombre, and they seemed to be leaving civilisation behind with every passing mile.

The sky was overcast, the threat of rain in the air, and Guy Chabrol seemed to have grown more cold and sombre too as they went further into this wilderness.

'I thought you had another château much closer to Paris, *Monsieur le Comte*?' Wanda Balfour said suddenly and, even in her aunt's voice, Lucy could hear a thread of alarm. She had also revealed the fact that she knew more about Guy Chabrol than she had led him to believe and, glancing at him quickly, Lucy saw his dark eyes narrow slightly. Here was a man who missed nothing at all. Alarm and suspicion came flooding back.

'I do,' he said flatly, his voice cold. 'All that you require is here though: the library, the family papers. It is at the Château de Rochaine that my family treasures rest and that, I think, is what you seek, *madame*?'

'Well, yes,' her aunt said, instantly back to enthusiasm. 'I can't do a lot without the books and papers.' She laughed merrily but Guy Chabrol did not smile. His eyes were hard and cold, watching the road, his carved lips in one straight line.

'Then you will be content, *madame*, I assure you, and so will I. In any case, we are almost there.'

They had been driving along between thick trees for some time, the road winding and quite narrow in places, nothing much to see. Now, without warning, they came out into the rather sullen light of a late sun, a great stretch of land before them that rose to a low hill. On the hill stood the Château de Rochaine and at the sight of it Lucy's heart leapt frighteningly and then sank.

It was much, much bigger than any of the places she had seen on the way. It seemed to be almost surrounded by water and, although it was beautiful, its turrets soaring, great towers at each corner, it looked nothing at all like the large country mansion she had wishfully imagined. It was a fortress, even in this age looking impregnable. It looked as cold and powerful as the man who owned it, the man who now turned to her with a wry look that came flashing to his face when he saw her expression.

'Welcome to the Château de Rochaine, my family home, Mademoiselle Balfour,' he said sardonically. 'It has repelled attack for centuries and is, I think, exactly what is needed now.'

'What—what do you mean?' Lucy asked quickly, looking up into two cold dark eyes.

'Surely I have explained, *mademoiselle*?' he murmured. 'Your aunt needs the use of the old library. It is housed here.'

'Of course that's what the count means, Lucinda!' Wanda suddenly said sharply. 'I wonder how you manage, really I do. Sometimes you can't even understand a few simple words.'

Normally such a totally unexpected remonstration would have had Lucy blushing, especially as it was delivered in front of this arrogant man. Right now, though, it just washed over her because her eyes were held by two dark eyes that looked straight back at her and what she saw there was disdain for her aunt, a disdain that had until now been hidden and aimed solely at herself. He wasn't fooled one bit and he did not need a history of his family. Such a family would have been catalogued over and over in the history of France itself. He had walked into no trap at all.

She tore her eyes away and looked at the great dark château, at the water that almost surrounded it, flat and silver-grey in the fading light, at the dark trees that edged the water, tall and old as the château itself. It was ridiculous, she assured herself. They would be perfectly free to leave whenever her aunt's research was over. Even so, she felt a cold shiver pass over her skin. If they would be free to leave then why did she feel so menaced, so captured?

She glanced at Guy Chabrol and saw the slight smile that edged his lips as he looked back at her.

'You have very alert instincts, *mademoiselle*,' he said
softly, his voice once again lowered to exclude Wanda.
'It is a gift given in excess to the innocent. Rest easy
though. You may not need to flee from this place. As I
have already informed you, *tout va bien*.'

Lucy thought not. Other phrases were ringing in her
head, not the least the one about there being plenty of
servants to guard her.

She tilted her chin proudly and looked right back at
him.

'I'm not at all uneasy, *monsieur*,' she told him sharply,
but his soft laughter, coming quite unexpectedly, informed her that she should be uneasy, very uneasy
indeed, and, as they set off again, their contemplation
of the château over, she could only agree.

That the château had once been a fortress was quite
clear as they came closer. It almost seemed to be floating
on water and from close up the stone walls were even
more daunting, towering over them. They crossed by a
many-arched bridge and then were driving beneath the
mighty walls as a wide gravelled drive led them to the
overpowering entrance.

'We have arrived,' Guy Chabrol said quietly, and Lucy
heard a great deal of satisfaction in that voice. Was it
imagination? She didn't really think so and, as they
stepped from the car and followed him into the château,
she vowed to keep her eyes wide open and all her instincts
well alert. Somehow she knew that this time her aunt
had made a very big mistake.

The next morning, Lucy stood in her bedroom feeling
greatly inclined to miss breakfast altogether. The night
before had been a sort of nightmare, a great trial because they were not at all welcome, a fact that did not
seem to penetrate the inner reaches of her aunt's mind.

Everything was larger than life. The rooms were high-ceilinged and too big. The passages were dark and long, the stairs too wide. It had been bad enough before dinner, but, as they had come down to meet the count's stepmother and sit at the huge dining table, Lucy had felt a wave of actual fury at the Comte de Chauvrais. He was toying with them for reasons of his own and he was about to make them as uncomfortable as possible. Left to herself she would even have walked back to Paris and somehow managed to get to England. Her aunt, though, seemed to be utterly oblivious to any atmosphere.

The servants had been sullen, polite but very much cold-faced and Véronique Chabrol, Comtesse de Chauvrais, had been icy enough to be called almost rude. They had gone down to the huge dining-room and had needed a servant to show them the way, Wanda dressed in her usual finery and Lucy once again in the blue dress.

It had been cold. There was heating but no amount of heating could have coped with this great place and every door and window had seemed to let in enough draught to convince anyone they had been left open.

It was ridiculous that four people should be seated at such a grand table and Véronique's expression led Lucy to believe that she was in agreement. Her face iced over even more as Wanda began to talk, a thing she did without any pause for breath, her voice fervent and eager until Lucy, well aware of the atmosphere, could have sunk into the floor.

The countess was beautifully dressed but it did not escape Lucy's notice that she wore a thick shawl around her shoulders and even then shivered from time to time. Lucy felt almost stiff with cold and everyone seemed to be glaring at them except the count, who was having a very good time, his dark eyes watchful and ironic as Wanda talked.

'You appear to come from a very talented family, *mademoiselle*,' the countess said politely during a small gap in Wanda's discourse. 'Your mother an artist, your father a poet and your aunt a writer. You are also talented?'

'I'm afraid not, *madame*,' Lucy said quietly. 'I don't seem to be gifted at all.' Véronique Chabrol looked as if she was greatly relieved to hear it but the count cut in in his ruthless way.

'Mademoiselle Balfour is a helper,' he murmured sardonically. 'She has ministered to her mother and father and now she does the same thing for her aunt. It is the normal function of the less talented when surrounded by gifted people is it not, *mademoiselle*?'

'I have no idea, *monsieur*,' Lucy said quietly, ignoring his insulting tone, and deciding to be prim. 'I've never lived close to anyone who did not profess some talent.'

'Lucinda wouldn't even know it if she had talent,' Wanda announced vigorously. 'She's always been willing to give her own life up for other people. It's the way she was brought up. She's such a mouse, aren't you, my dear?'

Wanda said it all with a smile, a steamroller as usual, her hand patting Lucy's cold fingers. Véronique Chabrol frowned quite alarmingly but the count simply regarded Lucy with ironic interest, not at all concerned that his remarks had led to this. In any case, she was too cold to blush. It was Véronique who took over firmly. A servant came in and handed a shawl to her and the countess promptly handed it on to the count.

'It takes no talent to freeze,' she said tartly. 'Pass this shawl to Mademoiselle Balfour, Guy. I assume you have not invited her here in order to watch her catch pneumonia in this draughty place?'

He didn't pass it on. Instead he got up and walked over to Lucy, carefully draping the shawl around her, his hands lingering on her slender shoulders.

'*Je suis vraiment désolé, mademoiselle,*' he murmured. 'I had not noticed that you were so cold.'

'I'm quite all right, thank you,' Lucy said quickly, wanting him to go away. He was very alarming close up and as he bent over her she had the frightened feeling that she was merely some pawn in a plan she knew nothing about. If every evening was to be like this then she would have to invent some excuse to stay out of it. She would have gladly called herself a servant and eaten with them but she didn't appear to be very popular in that direction either.

She looked out of the window now, though, and had her first glimpse of the surrounding countryside in real daylight. It was certainly beautiful and there was no sign of any other building at all. The Château de Rochaine gazed menacingly out across the softly wooded hills and, looking down at the surrounding water in the morning sunlight, Lucy could see that it was quite deep, probably the old moat, because there was no doubt at all that this had been a fortress and to her it seemed to be one now, a place of captivity.

There was a sharp knock on her door and, when she answered it, Lucy found herself facing Guy Chabrol. He was leaning elegantly against the deep frame of the door and his eyes captured hers instantly. He was wearing a sporty-looking jacket and tan trousers, a high-necked white sweater making him look darker than ever, and he seemed to be in a good mood.

'I have come to escort you to breakfast, *mademoiselle.*'

His eyes moved, slipping over her coolly, as he made this announcement. This morning she was not about to be caught out as she had been last night. She was wearing a thick jumper and a tweedy skirt, another short one as she didn't possess a skirt that was both long and warm.

He just went on looking at her, summing her up, and she felt almost hypnotised. He was very annoying and her lips tightened crossly.

'Thank you,' she managed. 'I should go to my aunt though.'

'Why? Do you also dress her? Surely she can manage to find her own clothes?' He took her arm to lead her off, infuriatingly arrogant.

'I don't dress her, *monsieur*. I merely thought she would never find her way downstairs in this place.'

'And you would?' he enquired derisively, ignoring her sharp tone and leading her on with no relaxing of his grip. 'You would probably have ended up in one of the towers and stayed there for weeks. In any case, I have dispatched a servant to bring your aunt down to breakfast.'

'The servant could have collected me too,' Lucy snapped, forgetting to be polite to their host in her fury at his arrogance. The moment he appeared he made her blood boil. He was so imperious, so effortlessly haughty!

'I was passing.' He shrugged dismissively and then looked down at her with something close to amusement. 'This morning you are less of a mouse, *mademoiselle*. You are transformed into a shrew?'

'You have no right to insult me, *monsieur*!' Lucy stopped and looked up at him angrily but he continued to regard her steadily, his dark eyes narrowed at this display of temper.

'You reserve that right for your aunt, *mademoiselle*? She is accustomed to sharpening her rather spiteful wits on you?'

Lucy looked up at him with enormous blue eyes. 'She's not spiteful. If you're talking about last night... She just doesn't think sometimes.'

'You mean, she opens her mouth and words fall out?'

'She gets very enthusiastic. If you have a bad opinion of her——'

'I keep my opinions to myself, *mademoiselle*.'

'Except when they're about me,' Lucy reminded him angrily. 'You despise me and you despise my aunt too. Why did you let her talk you into having us here?'

'I do not let anyone talk me into anything, *mademoiselle*,' he said quietly, staring down at her. 'Surely your aunt is famous? It is very good to have my family catalogued for the future by such a woman, *n'est-ce pas*?'

'You know perfectly well that she's not famous,' Lucy accused. 'Your family are probably written into French history. Even if they weren't, you wouldn't have chosen my aunt. Someone like you would have chosen a really famous person who would have been honoured to do it.'

'Honoured? You flatter me, *mademoiselle*. I understand from your aunt that she has written about many families of the French nobility, some of whom I know. You are telling me that she is a fraud?'

'I'm not telling you anything,' Lucy fumed. 'I'm just suspicious.'

'Ah! You imagine that I am Bluebeard? I assure you that if I had been so inclined I would have gone about it in the usual way. Let us proceed.' His hand came back to her arm but Lucy sprang away.

'Please don't touch me!'

The amusement died from his eyes and Lucy felt colour flare under her skin.

'I am merely being polite,' he assured her quietly. 'Do not be afraid of me. I would not like that.'

'I'm not afraid of you,' Lucy lied gallantly, her head tossed back.

'Then control your trembling legs and we will proceed.' His hand came back to her arm and she didn't seem to have any alternative.

'You have read your aunt's books?' he enquired after a while when they seemed to be still nowhere near the lower rooms.

'One,' she informed him briefly, not prepared to give an inch.

'Yes, one would probably be enough,' he murmured scathingly, changing the subject then with ease. 'You slept well?'

'Hardly at all, *monsieur*. I was cold.'

'Once again, I am desolate, *mademoiselle*. Tonight I will arrange for you to be warm. I do not intend to punish you.'

'Punish me? Why should you do that?' Lucy swung round again to face him as they reached the vast, tiled hall and he looked down at her wryly, his well-delineated lips curved downwards in amusement.

'It was perhaps a lack of understanding of your language,' he said smoothly. 'I am wondering, *mademoiselle*, why I am at the receiving end of this temper of yours today. Perhaps it is because you have spent a cold and uncomfortable night? I must see that it does not happen again. You are much more acceptable as a mouse.'

He pushed open a door and she had no time to reply because both the countess and her aunt were already there and the sight of them seemed to bring her to her senses. How had she dared speak to Guy Chabrol like that? She shot him a worried look and then hastily got on with her breakfast. He was busy watching her intently, so intently that he didn't answer when her aunt spoke to him. Wanda had to say the same thing twice but that never bothered her; she had a certain expertise in that line.

Véronique Chabrol frowned on everyone and then an old butler came in and frowned too. The count kept on staring at her and she shrank into her easiest role. It was definitely safer to be a mouse. She would have to try and remember that.

Breakfast over, the count seemed to be determined that work would begin at once.

'I will show you the old library,' he informed her aunt. 'It is on the ground floor and quite close so you will have no trouble finding your way about. A few days and you will also be able to negotiate the passages to your rooms. I assume, *madame*, that this work will take some considerable time?'

Lucy was interested. A similar question from herself to her aunt had brought forth a strange smile and a strange reply. This time, though, Wanda was quite straightforward.

'It will depend on the books, *monsieur*, and the papers. If everything necessary is there I will be able to read and take notes with some speed. Lucinda and I will not be in your way for very long. She is a good typist and——'

'You are not in my way, *madame*,' he said quietly. 'I am very happy to have you here. It is a great stroke of good fortune. As to your niece, I find Mademoiselle Balfour quite charming.'

Lucy didn't know which one of them looked at him with the greatest suspicion; her aunt, his stepmother or herself. The count, however, looked at Lucy, that certain indefinable something once again at the back of those stunning dark eyes, and she was very glad to follow her aunt as he led the way to the library.

It was situated on a long dark passage—a feature that seemed to dominate the château—but once inside the darkness disappeared. The floor was covered in brilliantly coloured tiles, the walls hung with old tapestries

which were still vivid despite their age. Sunlight streamed
in at the windows, giving the old room a very airy
appearance, and, although Wanda immediately turned
to the books with an almost zealous speed, Lucy stood
and looked round the room, admiring it, her eyes going
to the long windows and then to the high ceiling, which
was wooden and painted with the colours that predom-
inated in the tapestries.

'You did not expect this, *mademoiselle*?' Guy Chabrol
asked quietly when he saw her smiling face.

'No,' she murmured truthfully. 'I expected darkness,
dust and a certain amount of decay.'

'*Mon Dieu!*' He looked at her in amused surprise. 'The
books are priceless. There is no decay, *mademoiselle*. I
am a financier and not exactly given to neglecting things
that are either valuable or works of art. You find the
château dirty and dusty? I will dismiss the servants.'

'I don't find the château either dirty or dusty,' Lucy
got out hastily. He looked capable of carrying out any
threat. Maybe that was why the servants looked so grim.
'It's very beautiful, though a little daunting. For me it's
just too big and too cold.'

'The cold can be remedied, *mademoiselle*. The size, I
am afraid, is a fact of life. You will become accustomed
to it.'

'We'll be gone, *monsieur*, before that happens,' Lucy
murmured hopefully, but he did not answer that remark,
and when she looked up his eyes were keenly on her aunt,
who was now completely silent, her glance riveted on
the old leather-bound books that lined the room to the
ceiling.

Halfway up the room a gallery with wrought-iron rails
made the upper books more accessible but, even so, the
room was so high and there were so many books that a
short ladder was necessary to reach the top of the lower
half.

'I will leave you to it, *madame*,' the count said quietly, and Lucy thought her aunt had not heard at all, for certainly she did not answer and Lucy answered for her.

'Thank you, *monsieur*.'

It gained her an ironic look. 'Ah! You are back in your role as professional shadow. You will not be disturbed here. Let me know if there is anything you need.'

Lucy turned to her aunt when the door had closed behind Guy Chabrol. By this time, Wanda was moving excitedly along the upper gallery, nothing on her mind but books.

'What do you want me to do, Aunt Wanda?' She had to speak twice before she gained her aunt's attention and then it was only vaguely given.

'Oh—er—nothing, Lucinda. I'll have to really look around before I know where to begin.' She stared down at Lucy as if she wasn't quite seeing her and then her eyes strayed to the sunlit windows. 'Er—we'll need good photographs for the illustrations. I never have them taken professionally. It's too expensive. You can make a start on that as we have such a sunny day. Yes, make a start on that, different angles of the château. There's a good camera in my room, top drawer by the bed.'

Wanda turned away and Lucy went on looking at her in surprise. It was quite clear that her aunt had forgotten that she was there at all. She had never thought that her aunt would be so involved with her work. The books she had written, if the one that Lucy had read was a normal example, were very superficial and did not look particularly well researched. As to the photographs, her own irritation as she had read her aunt's book and seen the illustrations was now explained. She went out into the passage, her mind pondering on it, a little frustrated frown on her face when she realised she would have to find her aunt's bedroom all by herself.

A very daunting-looking woman materialised out of
the shadows and Lucy pounced on her, searching quickly
for her few words of French.

'Er—*la chambre de Madame Balfour, s'il vous plâit*,'
she managed with a firmness that came mostly from
anxiety at the idea of being lost in this great place and
ending up in one of the towers that Guy Chabrol had
spoken of.

All she got for a moment was a haughty look.

'I am Madame Gatien, the housekeeper, *mademoiselle*. I speak English. I will get a servant to escort you
and bring you back down should you wish it.'

Lucy wondered what the difference was in this haughty
woman's mind between being a servant and being a
housekeeper. She just nodded her thanks, though, and
followed a very tight-faced girl upstairs to her aunt's
room. Why were they all so angry-looking? They
probably took their cue from the count. The château
wasn't the only thing here that was cold!

It wasn't cold outside. With the camera over her
shoulder Lucy made her way to the front of the château
and walked across the wide, gravelled drive. She leaned
over the balustrade and looked down at the water,
shivering a little when she saw how still it was, how deep-
looking, and she was glad to move away.

She began to look around for possible shots, the sun
warm on her arms through the sweater she wore. It was
much better out here than in the château and it would
be a good idea to make the most of it. She wandered
round the side of the building, still stunned at its size,
but her enthusiasm for her new occupation growing by
the minute.

It was not easy to take shots so close to such a mighty
structure and she wandered well away from it, intrigued
when her eyes fell on a square block of buildings some
small distance from the château itself. A few photo-

graphs from there would be useful; perhaps if she climbed one of the walls by the stone steps she would see it from a better angle. Besides, she was now in an exploring mood and it was a good excuse.

A walk across a cobbled courtyard and a narrow field brought her to the foot of the white walls and she began to climb carefully up the stone steps cut into the side. It was a bit tricky and she had to cling to the wall. They were not now as secure as they had been centuries ago— many were crumbling—but she managed quite well and stopped halfway up to survey the scene. Shots from here would be reasonably good. She was determined to produce something more professional than her aunt seemed to achieve.

Before she had time to get the camera out of its case, however, a noise had her almost freezing into stillness, her heart beginning to pound frantically as Guy Chabrol came out of the building leading a horse, his earlier outfit discarded for riding gear, only the white high-necked sweater the same.

Lucy flattened herself against the wall, hoping he wouldn't notice her. It now seemed to be a very odd thing to do, to climb this wall and cling there, and she could imagine what he would say in that sardonic voice if he saw her. She felt guilty and foolish, irritated beyond words that she had landed herself in this situation and she pressed against the wall more tightly, almost hovering over him, hardly daring to breathe.

It was not her lucky day. He glanced up as he was preparing to mount and stopped abruptly, his eyes widening in surprise as he saw her suspended halfway up the wall, so very obviously hiding. She couldn't think of a thing to say and he just went on staring up at her, saying nothing whatever until her face flushed painfully and she started to come back down, to explain her odd behaviour. But the shock of seeing him and her very precarious footing combined to make her slip, panic on her face as she felt herself falling.

He moved fast, catching her as she slid from the wall, her impetus knocking them both to the ground rather alarmingly near to the irritated horse. Lucy felt unable to move, all the breath knocked from her even though his arms had caught her and he had taken the full impact of the fall.

He made no attempt to move. For a second he just lay there staring up at the sky and then he turned his head to stare at her as she rested uneasily half across his body. It was a very powerful body, packed with taut muscle, and breathing became more difficult still as she looked into his narrowed eyes. She was sure he was trying not to laugh and it made things much worse. It was a great relief when he decided to speak.

'I ask myself what is wrong with you, *mademoiselle*? I give consideration to the idea that there is insanity in your family,' he murmured, his dark brows raised quizzically. 'Your behaviour is often strange but, now, you surpass yourself. You think that like the mouse you can run up a wall, eh?'

His eyes moved slowly over her face, searching for some sign of mental instability in every feature, apparently, and Lucy looked at him warily.

'I—I was going to take a photograph.' Her breath wasn't quite her own yet and it became even more unsteady as he moved slowly, his body brushing her own. He lowered her to the ground, resting on one elbow to look down at her, studying her face.

'You were not then poised to attack me from this advantageous position?' His dark eyes were filled with ironic amusement and she found herself looking right into them from an alarmingly intimate situation.

'Of—of course not. I was photographing the château. It's not too easy from close up.'

It wasn't too easy being close up to Guy Chabrol either. His skin was lightly tanned, subtly darker than an English skin, and now that she was so near she could see that his eyes were very dark brown and not black at all. He had thick eyelashes and his mouth was long, sensuous, and, at the moment, not so cruel-looking as usual. Of course, that was because he was laughing at her and not in his usual disdainful frame of mind for some unfathomable reason. He seemed to find this all very amusing even though he had taken a fall with her on top of him.

He looked down at her for a few more seconds, his eyes narrowed and intent, and sparks of feeling began to tear into her, making her face pale. A shiver raced over her skin as his eyes burned into hers. There was something frighteningly familiar about him, as if she had known him long ago. A flush seemed to cover her whole body, invisible but burning, and a strange little sound welled up in her throat.

He suddenly stood with unbelievably smooth, graceful movement, reaching to pull her to her feet. It brought her to her senses. The dazed feeling vanished and she was utterly flustered, wondering what had happened to her then. She felt as if she had been somewhere else, lost in time. It must have been the shock of the fall.

'I'm sorry if I hurt you when I fell on you.'

'You did not fall on me, *mademoiselle*. I caught you. As to your weight, it seems not to be there at all. Does Madame Balfour starve you? Is this why you are so slight?'

His lips twisted in amusement that was not now so benign and Lucy was back to embarrassment, wishing him miles away.

'I come from a very thin family.'

'Hmm,' he murmured scathingly, his glance flaring over her. 'I have only observed one other member of your family. From my observation of her I would very much doubt it.' His eyes slid over her face, lingering on the high cheekbones that were very pronounced. 'Your aunt is remarkably well cared for, *mademoiselle. You* are all eyes. We must feed you up and observe you later.'

'I won't be here long enough for any experiments,' Lucy snapped, colour rising under her skin. She hadn't felt at all odd until she had met Guy Chabrol. The long lips quirked, back to cruelty or very close to it.

'That, I would imagine, will depend upon how quickly your aunt discovers what she is seeking.'

It was a funny way of putting things and Lucy looked at him firmly. 'She's busy right now, Monsieur Chabrol. She's enthralled by the books.'

His eyebrows rose, though whether at her sharp tone or her remarks she couldn't say. 'You have decided then that I am to be *monsieur* and not *le comte*?' he queried mockingly.

'You said you didn't use the title,' Lucy reminded him, wondering if she had made a big social mistake but not too bothered.

'I said that the title was now worthless,' he corrected. 'You are quite right though, I rarely use it, unless I wish to impress someone who irritates me.'

'Then you should use it with me,' Lucy said crossly, annoyed at being tied into knots by his ready tongue.

'But you do not irritate me, *mademoiselle*. I am merely astonished at your peculiarities.' He looked down at her for a second and then smiled to himself sardonically, some thought running through his mind that she could not fathom. He was a very unfathomable man, after all, and she would be very glad to get away from here and see the last of him.

'You need photographs of the château?' he murmured. '*Alors!* I will escort you.'

'Thank you, there's no need——' Lucy began until his amused tone stopped her.

'But there are so many walls, Mademoiselle Balfour. With your odd behaviour, I fear for you.' He picked up the reins of his now calm horse. 'Come. I will show you a good place for a photograph. It will be something for you to remember.'

CHAPTER THREE

THERE didn't seem to be any way of getting out of it, and Lucy walked silently beside the count as he led his horse away from the building and headed out towards the thick woods that lay beyond further fields.

'I didn't realise there were stables here.' Lucy glanced back at the white buildings and he stopped, turning to look back also.

'The château was built in the fifteenth century. It was not then as big as it is now but it was still very forbidding, a fortress. As it was used to house soldiers too, it required stables. Coaches were also kept there. It is now partially a museum, the coaches well-preserved.'

'Really? Can I see inside it?'

Lucy looked up at him hopefully and he nodded, his eyes slipping over her.

'Whenever you wish, but I must take you. Normally the place is locked. At the moment I am keeping my horse there but it will only be for a while.'

'Where do you usually keep it?' She stroked her hand down the sleek neck of the animal and he looked at her sharply.

'You are not afraid? I would have thought that something of this size would terrify you.'

'I've spent most of my life in the country,' Lucy said simply. 'I'm not afraid of horses. Where do you usually keep the horse?' she persisted.

'I have another château.'

He was brief to the point of surliness and Lucy glanced at him out of her eye corners. He was quite intriguing when you came to look at things closely. She had thought he was walking straight into her aunt's trap but he had not been doing any such thing. He was waiting instead as if he had a trap of his own to spring. Luckily she was beginning to get the feeling that she was merely on the edge of things.

His glance flashed across and he caught her looking at him but her thoughts were so absorbed that she looked straight back, not even flushing as she had done so often with this disdainful Frenchman.

'What about your photographs?'

The dark eyes held hers and she came swiftly back to the present, aware now that she had been staring and that her skin was tingling in a very odd manner again.

'I—I'll do it from here.' She turned away flustered, looking back at the château to escape from looking at him, and for a moment he came to stand by her, the reins looped over his arm.

'Shots from this distance are best, if the camera is up to it and if it was not damaged by the fall,' he murmured. 'Why do you wish to take photographs like some tourist?'

'Aunt Wanda asked me to. She wanted them for her book.'

'Really?' He looked very grim for a moment but then seemed to relent, his peculiar humour resurfacing. 'If you make a nonsense of them will she beat you?'

'I won't make a nonsense of them!' Lucy snapped, looking up at him irritably. 'I get on very well with my aunt and I know how to take photographs, thank you. I may not be talented but I'm not quite stupid!'

To her surprise he grinned down at her, his eyes moving over her pale face and her angry eyes.

'I begin to realise that you are a mouse who retaliates when attacked. I must try to remember that.'

'I'm not a mouse!' Lucy informed him crossly.

'Then why do you permit your aunt to bully you? I would have thought that you would fear me more.'

'She doesn't bully me! I've just told you that I get on very well with her. I suppose you mean last night at dinner? She didn't really mean any harm.'

'No? It is not the first time that I have heard her say sweetly disparaging things about you. She even sent you to bed at the hotel.'

'You were the one who was unforgivably rude last night,' Lucy pointed out hotly. 'As to the hotel, I was very glad to go to bed.' He just stared at her deeply and she looked away hastily; her temper was running away with her again. Pretty soon he would order them out of here and tell her aunt that she was to blame. It might be wise to humour him. 'In any case,' she added quickly, 'you don't understand about my family. Talented people tend to be a bit difficult. They expect to be spoiled and to say anything they wish.'

'Indeed? They pointed this out to you when you were very young so that you would know your place?'

'No, they didn't. I just grew up knowing it.'

'You say that you are not stupid. Why then did you not break free? Your aunt told me that your parents died. Did you feel the need to move into further servitude?'

'It's not servitude! I gave up my job deliberately to take this one with my aunt. I'm not trained for anything. I can't do anything except type a little. My aunt rescued me from... She offered me the chance to...'

'To what?' He looked down at her steadily with narrowed eyes, obviously going over her words in his mind, and she felt suddenly subdued. Why had she told this arrogant man about her problems? It was because he goaded her and she rose to the bait like an idiot instead of telling him to mind his own business. Clearly she *was* stupid or she would have kept her lips firmly closed and played a quiet role as she had planned to do.

'To—to see France—and help her.'

He changed the subject, obviously tiring of hearing about her drab life, his eyes moving over the sombre spectacle of his property.

'From inside, the view from the upper rooms of the east tower is magnificent. You can see the Loire and many miles beyond.'

'Do you like it here?' Lucy asked, greatly pleased to be reprieved.

'*Dieu!* I do not!' He turned and swung into the saddle. 'I will leave you to it, *mademoiselle*. I do not think you can come to much harm unless you deliberately seek danger. I will see you later.'

He just turned and cantered off across the soft grass and she watched him until the horse entered the woods and moved out of sight. It was easy to make up dreams about the Comte de Chauvrais, easy to imagine him dressed from some older time as he rode across the open fields and into the old woods.

Dreams about him would tend to be cold though and probably violent, because, although he had shown no sign of rage as yet, she was sure that it lurked below the surface. At the moment he had the air about him of someone who was hunting. His every action was calculated and alert. He was a very worrying man and she would be glad when her aunt had finished here and they could go.

She turned to the château again and began to take photographs. He obviously hated being here. So why had he come? Why was he indulging her aunt when he so clearly despised her? She pushed the thoughts away but she could not rid her mind of the thought of Guy Chabrol. His dark, sardonic face was printed firmly in front of her and she had the really astonishing thought that she would never be able to forget him. The coldly handsome face seemed to be too deeply etched into her mind.

She stayed out as long as she could and only just managed to find her way back by lunchtime. Her aunt had not missed her and only answered vaguely when Lucy spoke. She was clearly well into her research and Lucy was glad. The sooner they left here the better as far as she was concerned.

They had the dining-room to themselves, their lunch served by the very old and very grim-looking butler. The Comtesse de Chauvrais was not there and Lucy felt a pang of something closely resembling disappointment when Guy Chabrol missed lunch too.

The room was still cold even though the sun was very warm outside and as her aunt left to go back to the library Lucy followed her thoughtfully. Why did she feel that the place was boring if that cool-faced man was not there? She supposed that he was the nearest thing to excitement she had ever had in her life. Calculating what he would do next was more exciting than all the rest of her life put together. She had never met a man like that before. He was as far above her very ordinary life as a dark-faced god.

As they entered the library her heart gave an uncomfortable leap as they encountered the count just leaving it. He gave a slight bow to her aunt and then looked at Lucy.

'You have your photographs, *mademoiselle*?' he asked politely.

'Yes, thank you.' She hoped he wouldn't taunt her about her odd actions of this morning and get her aunt interested. He didn't. He simply nodded to her too and walked off, but Wanda stood and stared after him.

'I wonder what he was doing in the library?' she mused, and Lucy looked at her in surprise.

'I expect he'll keep an eye on us. The library is full of treasures.'

'How would you know, dear?' Wanda asked with a burst of amusement.

Lucy felt a spark of rebellion, and was quite pleased to be able to say, 'The count told me.'

Wanda looked extremely interested, but she didn't say anything and, once again, Lucy was intrigued. Crossing swords with Guy Chabrol seemed to have brought her to life and she noticed that her aunt's voice was a little flustered as she handed a notebook across and murmured, 'You'd better take a few notes. Follow me around. I'll dictate. I'll start with a list of the books I've already decided to use.'

As they were in French and as Lucy did not speak the language it proved to be a pointless exercise, an exercise that ended up as a sort of trail around the room with Wanda pointing and Lucy carefully copying titles. Wanda was finding her something to do. She knew that for sure. So why had her aunt brought her here and paid for her keep at that expensive hotel? Of course, Guy Chabrol had paid in the end, but Wanda was not to have known he would be so chivalrous. It would have been cheaper to leave Lucy back in England at her own job.

Was her aunt disparaging? No, she just spoke without thought as her parents had often done. It was the artistic nature perhaps? Guy Chabrol was making her suspicious of everything and everyone. He was the villain if there was one. She realised impatiently that she was looking at her aunt with entirely new eyes, expecting sinister happenings. It was this great place and the dark, daunting master of it. She would do well to keep suspicion right at the top of her mind as far as he was concerned.

*   *   *

Over the next few days it became very obvious to Lucy that Guy Chabrol was really playing some game of his own. He was as silent as ever but there was an air of waiting about him that kept her nerves on edge. Even the servants appeared to be waiting, none of them seeming quite at home in the place, their sullen looks not abating at all.

Wanda apparently noticed nothing whatever. She was utterly absorbed with the books and merely finding jobs for Lucy to do. Lucy was quite touched by it. It became clearer every day that her aunt had merely been rescuing her from her dull life. Sometimes she was unable to find anything at all and then Lucy was free to roam out of doors in the continuing good weather, to explore the outer perimeters of the château.

She took her courage firmly in hand and faced Guy Chabrol one day as she found him also out of doors.

'You said I could see the old stables, *monsieur*,' she reminded him with a smile, subduing her resentment of him to get her own way. His dark eyes rested on her face. The smile seemed to have brought sunlight into it, the blue of her eyes deepening. He stared at her and then nodded and simply turned in the direction of the stables.

'No time like the present, *mademoiselle*. Let us go there now.'

'I hope I'm not interrupting anything——' Lucy started apologetically, but he cut in before she could go on.

'There is nothing to interrupt. I am simply waiting. I think that perhaps you and I wait together but for different reasons.'

'I'm not waiting for anything,' Lucy assured him blithely, still congratulating herself on having wheedled him into doing what she wanted.

'In which case, why are you so free at this moment? You are what the English call "at a loose end", *n'est-ce pas*?'

'Well, at the moment,' she admitted reluctantly. 'There's nothing for me to do in the library.'

'I am amazed that there ever is anything for you to do, *mademoiselle*. You do not speak French. The books are in French. Your position as helper seems to be very limited.'

'When my aunt starts with her notes I'll be invaluable.' Lucy looked at him firmly but to her surprise his lips quirked and he glanced down at her as she walked along beside him, a slender girl with fine, delicate bone-structure.

'And what is she doing now? I would have thought that the note-taking would have begun.'

'Oh, she's still looking through the books. After all, there are so many. I don't think she's got what she wants yet.'

'Neither do I, Mademoiselle Balfour. You see, we are in agreement. It is quite possible to get on well together.' There was a little warmth in the amusement this time and Lucy stopped to look at him but he urged her onwards, his hand against her back. 'The stables,' he reminded quietly. 'Let us make the most of your free time.'

They had come to the square stable block and Lucy stopped abruptly. It was quite dark inside. He switched on lights, his face amused as he glanced at her.

'Modern facilities, *mademoiselle*. An attack of nerves is not necessary. Allow me to show you around.'

Her small feeling of superiority fled. He could reduce her to size with one glance but she was determined to enjoy this unexpected treat.

There were stalls for horses, but only one was now there, the chestnut horse that the count had brought here with him. The harness-room smelled of leather and the

old tackle there was still in very fine condition. Obviously
this place was considered to be worthwhile and as they
moved to the coach-house she saw why.

There were five coaches, all very uncomfortable-
looking but all well-preserved. It was like being back in
time and she looked longingly at the most elaborate one,
startled when the count suddenly said, 'Step inside. Be
a countess for one brief moment.' He opened the car-
riage door and handed her in before she could protest,
and, although she felt a trifle foolish, she was thrilled
as she sat on the quilted seat, a smile edging her lips.

'Impressive,' he murmured mockingly. 'With a little
attention to your appearance and a little more poise you
would pass as the real thing.'

'On a very dark night,' Lucy muttered, the pleasure
wiped from her face.

'I have offended you?' He blocked her way as she
made an attempt to get out. 'I assure you that my remarks were complimentary. Have I not tried to make
you comfortable here in the château?'

'Not terribly,' Lucy said clearly, trying to edge past
him. 'I know perfectly well that you're laughing at me
all the time, however polite your face. I also know that
you don't like either my aunt or me.'

'Your innocent instincts are working overtime,' he
assured her softly, the dark eyes gleaming. 'I admit to
not liking your aunt but have I not already said that I
find you charming? I even said it in front of your aunt
and my stepmother.'

'You didn't mean it, and why should you? It was just
another way of getting at me to amuse yourself.'

To her consternation he lifted her out, his hands
staying firmly around her tiny waist.

'You are unkind to me, *mademoiselle*. Also you are
not very grateful. Think of the things I have done for
you. I have saved you from a nasty fall when you climbed

the wall with your camera. I have brought you here the very first time you mentioned it but, most of all, I have seen to it that you are warm and cosy at night. You have never thanked me at all.'

Lucy looked up at him guiltily. After her complaint that she had slept badly because she was cold, there had been a fire in her room each night, the cheerful blaze making her comfortable. It was quite true that she hadn't once thanked him.

'I—I'm sorry,' she pleaded softly. 'I wanted to thank you but each time I've seen you my aunt has been there and I didn't know if...'

'You didn't know if I had ordered the same comforts for her?' he prompted. 'I have not. In the first place, she did not complain of the cold. She is so eager to be here that I believe she would have been content had the roof been removed. In the second place, as you so astutely remarked, I do not like her. I am grateful for your consideration in not speaking about it in front of her. You may thank me now.'

'Th-thank you,' Lucy said tremulously. 'It was very kind and I find the blaze cheerful.'

The powerful hands tightened on her waist and she was securely trapped, her back against the old coach. He seemed to be towering over her and a very queer excitement began to shiver through her, making her lower her eyes and look down as he watched her intently. In here he seemed more like a dark god than ever; an exciting alien air about him, the tilt of his head, the firm, carved lips.

'Very nice words,' he mocked softly. 'I prefer deeds. I will be quite satisfied if you kiss me for the favours I am bestowing on you while everyone else freezes.'

'I—I don't understand... I... You can't say that...'

Lucy was shocked into looking up and his hand captured her face like a butterfly in a net, keeping it turned to his.

'Why not? You owe me thanks. That is all the thanking I require. One kiss.'

'No! Please, no!' Panic welled up in Lucy and she tried to move but his arm tightened around her waist and the hand on her face was firm, keeping it tilted to his.

'You are too much of a mouse to kiss a man?' he jeered quietly, and Lucy's blue eyes flashed sparks of resentment. This was merely to amuse himself, a very chauvinistic way of amusing himself. He had no intention of kissing her.

'Yes!' she snapped, looking up at him angrily. 'In any case, I don't kiss people I hate!'

'Then I will kiss you,' he murmured. 'There is very little timidity in me and no hatred at all.'

Lucy struggled frantically but she had no chance to free herself. His arm was like an iron band and the long sensuous lips closed over her own, the warm hand on her face sliding into her hair.

She was completely unprepared, because even though he had been speaking like that she had not really believed it to the very last second. She had imagined this to be merely another of his taunts. It was no such thing. He was kissing her thoroughly, his arms tightening as she gasped and tried to escape.

'Relax. *Tout va bien*, little mouse,' he murmured in amusement against her parted lips. 'There is nothing to fear. You have never been kissed before? It is not a dangerous occupation.'

It was. His mouth caught hers swiftly and feeling began to flood her whole body as he deepened the kiss, drawing her tightly into warm, strong arms. She had never been held like that before, never felt this sort of response, never felt so wrapped up in warmth and pleasure. Fear left her as she softened, her face tilted of its own accord. His mouth opened over hers, draining her sweetness with sensuous, drowsy movements as his hands moulded her closer.

She was aware that the boys who had kissed her before were not at all experienced, something that had never occurred to her when she had found their kisses utterly unexciting. Now she felt in danger but her inner urges were to step more deeply into it.

She was trembling and silent when he lifted his head to look down at her flushed face. There was a burning response inside her that shocked her into silence. She was leaning softly against him, subdued and willing.

'You learn quickly,' he murmured. 'You tremble in my arms, melt to me. Perhaps this is your talent?'

Lucy began to come back to life, stunned at her own lack of resistance, but he went on before she could do anything, his hand coming to stroke her hair from her hot face.

'You look better with colour. Your skin is soft, your hair smells of shampoo and you smell of sweet soap, like a baby. With a little perfume, a trip to the hairdresser's and a few hours at the beauty salon, you would look almost human.'

The cruelly contemptuous words snapped her out of the hazy cloud she had been floating on and she came to earth with a bang, her trembling more pronounced, her eyes threatening to fill with tears.

'You think I have some redeeming features, then, *monsieur*?' she managed through trembling lips. 'Unfortunately, I can't say the same for you. You're cruel, rude and insensitive. If this is the result of being an aristocrat then I'm quite content to be a mouse!'

She pushed free of him and marched off towards the door, her eyes so filled with tears of humiliation that she tripped in the shadows cast by the dim lights and fell headlong, banging her knee painfully.

He was beside her instantly, helping her to her feet and then glaring down at her knee, which was cut and already beginning to bleed.

'*Dieu!*' he muttered through clenched teeth. 'You are the most guileless, feather-headed creature I have ever had the misfortune to meet. How that woman expects you to assist her here is quite beyond me. Looking at you is like looking into a piece of clear glass. Everything is visible.'

'I don't wish to be clever and subtle,' Lucy assured him with a catch in her voice. 'It might mean I had to be like you. I'll just go on being stupid.'

'As you have no alternative, that is a good decision,' he snapped, swinging her into his arms and walking out into the sunlight.

'You can put me down,' she ordered tearfully, but he didn't even look at her, he simply continued towards the château, his dark face tight and annoyed.

'Please put me down,' she begged more quietly. 'People will see me coming.'

'And no doubt they will hide,' he muttered sarcastically. 'In future I will do the same thing. As to people, I employ all of them. They think what I tell them to think and if they do not then they have sufficient intelligence to keep quiet. My stepmother already knows that I am a law unto myself. As to your aunt, at this moment I hope for her sake that we do not encounter her.'

They didn't, and Lucy found herself carried right up to her own room, very thankful that in this huge place they had met nobody at all. She sat still on the chair by the bed when he ordered her to do just that and he came in after a minute with a bowl of water and a cloth, bathing her knee even though she protested.

'You will keep still and be silent,' he rasped. 'I brought this about. I will correct it.'

'I fell over in the dim light,' she began but he looked up at her furiously as he knelt and began to bandage her leg.

'You fell over in a panic because I kissed you,' he corrected.

'That—that's ridiculous,' she stammered. 'I—I've been kissed before.'

'Like that?' His eyes flashed to her pale face. 'I doubt it! And I would not attempt lies were I you,' he muttered harshly as she opened her mouth. 'As I have told you, you have no subtlety.' He stood and surveyed his handiwork and then glanced at her sardonically. 'You may, however, say in the future with truth that you have been kissed.'

Lucy dared not look higher than her knee.

'You've done the bandaging very well,' she said in little more than a whisper and his angry eyes came back to her knee and the white bandage.

'Like you, I am not afraid of horses,' he bit out. 'I have done my fair share of seeing to their needs. Fillies also have long slender legs. The principle is the same.'

He walked out before she could start blushing and her door was closed with a certain amount of violence. Guy Chabrol was beginning to show just what lay beneath that cold exterior. He was dangerous. Even so, Lucy still felt how warm his arms had been, how persuasive his lips. She had been quite willing to stay there and be kissed after all. Her face flooded with colour when she realised that. Maybe she was as clear as glass? Maybe she was as stupid as he thought too? And why was he so angry with her aunt when he had invited her here himself? She stayed in her room and nobody missed her at all. It was like being on a rather weird holiday.

* * *

She tried to avoid him each day after that, playing a quiet role when she was forced to meet him at dinner or other meals, ducking her head to avoid the intent gaze he turned on her and speaking only when necessary. She was well aware that his stepmother considered her to be dull and entirely lacking in any sort of social grace but it mattered not at all. Each day was spent in avoiding the count as best she could.

It was only by silence she could manage it, because he seemed to spend a great deal of time wandering about and popping into the old library when he was least expected. The fact seemed to agitate her aunt too and she found plenty of work for Lucy, note-taking and searching for specific books.

The job was boring because almost everything her aunt dictated seemed to be sparse and uninteresting, not at all notes for some work that she hoped to sell. Nevertheless it did mean that Lucy was able to keep her head down and her face turned away when Guy Chabrol sauntered into the room. She began to breathe more easily when he was about—and that was a mistake.

'Get that green book for me, Lucinda,' her aunt ordered one afternoon. 'It's the small leather-bound one at the end of the top row there.'

She pointed to the higher books, those that needed a ladder to be reached, and Lucy located it, moving the ladder and climbing up to get it as her aunt watched.

'This one?' She leaned across and Wanda's voice came very quickly.

'Yes. It's the only green one on that row. Be careful. It's probably priceless. Don't drop it whatever you do.' She gave a sort of small gasp and then her tone changed like magic. 'Oh, good afternoon, *monsieur*,' she murmured, and, even if she hadn't, Lucy would have known that Guy Chabrol was in the room, again unexpectedly.

He was able to unsettle her by doing very little and the mere fact of his being suddenly there made her feel shaken. Her desire to get down the ladder became urgent. She was wearing another short skirt and as usual it made her very conscious of her appearance, especially as she was stuck up at the top of the ladder.

She made a grab for the book and missed, the rather violent action making the ladder sway and a small sound of alarm left her lips when it came away from the shelves. It seemed to be about to slide sideways and Lucy hung on to the shelves, knowing that she was about to be left dangling there in a very ungainly position.

The ladder was steadied and held firmly in place and she looked down rather fearfully to see the count gazing up at her in ironic surprise.

'Pardon my intervention, *mademoiselle*,' he murmured sardonically. 'I thought you were about to fall. Clearly, though, you are well able to look after yourself and not accustomed to requiring aid.'

His dark eyes were amused and Lucy made a very hasty descent of the ladder. She felt flushed and dusty and it did nothing to make her feel better when he grasped her arm and turned to her aunt.

'I would like to borrow your helper for a few moments, *madame*,' he said coolly. 'If you have no objection I will take her with me now.'

'Of course, *monsieur*!'

It was clear that her aunt wanted him out of the library with all speed but her eyes were very suspicious as she looked at Lucy. Suspicion was on Lucy's mind too but hers was more of a certainty. He was himself at 'a loose end' and wanted to do a little goading. She turned on him as the door shut behind them.

'If you wanted to speak to me about being stupid, then don't bother,' she snapped. 'I know all about it. If you hadn't been there I would have fallen again. Thank you for saving me. Goodbye!'

She made to walk off but his hand closed around her arm tightly and he turned her in the other direction.

'I am not about to tease you, *mademoiselle*. I wish to hold a very civilised conversation with you. I enjoy taking care of you and I do not mind at all that I am constantly catching you as you fall, or picking you up after the event. You have thanked me very nicely and——'

'I'm not thanking you in any other way,' Lucy announced, suspicion back on her face.

'After last time, I wouldn't dream of it,' he assured her drily. 'The aftermath was very painful for you and very irritating for me. I see that your leg is nicely healed,' he added, glancing down at her. 'Does it hurt now?'

She didn't deign to answer that. 'What do you want to talk about?' She set her feet firmly and stopped right where she was.

'I am about to have coffee. I have ordered tea for you. I intend to be very courteous. There is nothing to be uneasy about. Come.'

She had very little alternative unless she wanted to make a scene, and she found herself being urged forward to a room further along the great corridor that led to the outside. She was surprised to find that it was small and reasonably cosy and looked around suspiciously. Like the rest of the château it looked as if it belonged to a museum, not at all the sort of place to live in. The furnishings were very old and obviously irreplaceable, just like the books in the library. Had this place belonged to her she would have locked it up and posted guards; she would definitely not have chosen to live here.

The whole place overwhelmed her. The count overwhelmed her too and she looked at him warily as a grimfaced Madame Gatien came in with tea and coffee. She was doing the work of a servant and Lucy had no doubts of her opinions in this direction. Her grim face warned Lucy that the blame was to be placed squarely on her shoulders.

'It is time that you and I had a quiet conversation,' Guy Chabrol said firmly as the housekeeper left the room and closed the door. 'I think that here you will be reasonably safe, providing that you remain seated. There are no steps to climb.'

'What do you want to talk about?' Lucy eyed him carefully, taking a sip from her tea. She was too filled with suspicion by this turn of events to make any comment about his sarcastic observations.

'I wish to know what your future plans are.' He looked at her determinedly. 'I assume, *mademoiselle*, that your position of "helper" is a very temporary post? What will you do when you arrive back in England?'

'I'll probably go on helping my aunt,' Lucy stated, gathering her courage and looking him in the eye. 'I've told you already that I haven't any training or qualifications. If she doesn't want any more help then I'll— think about it. There are other jobs.'

'Why have you no qualifications?' he persisted. 'Your parents were trained, surely, and you are intelligent. You were lazy at school?'

'I didn't go to school at all until I was fourteen!' Lucy snapped, exasperation flooding through her. 'My father was originally a teacher and I was kept at home to study there. They didn't want me to—to mix with other children. They had very set ideas.'

His eyebrows rose sharply as he watched her rebellious face. 'They were not in trouble with the authorities for this unusual conduct?' he enquired wryly.

'All the time,' Lucy muttered, looking away from the dark intensity of his eyes. 'My father maintained he had the right to teach me at home though and he managed to make the battle last a very long time. It was a tricky point of law.'

'I would imagine it was trickier still for you. How did you manage to fit in studies between your duties as helper?'

'Quite easily,' Lucy informed him crossly. She was tired of his attitude. He just sat there and questioned her, his eyes coldly on her face as if she were a freak. 'The house was always full of people. Artists, poets, writers. I picked up a lot of information.'

'And yet you are neither an artist, a poet nor a writer?'

'I haven't any talent! I finally took a dull job and did it in a dull way!' Lucy snapped sarcastically.

'They reared you to be an oddity,' he stated firmly, looking very pleased with his conclusions, and Lucy glared at him, putting her cup down and preparing to walk out of this 'civilised conversation'.

'More of an oddity than you imagine, *monsieur*! I liked the flowers, the birds, the animals. I like to be free. Until I was thirteen I wore no shoes at all. I don't remember possessing any. I never wanted any.'

'Which may explain why now you frequently fall over your own feet,' he cut in smartly.

'If you've quite finished, *monsieur*?'

'I have not.' He signalled her back to her seat when she jumped up angrily. 'I now know more about you. I understand why you are very different from other people. 'You are strange—old-fashioned, *n'est-ce pas*? It does not trouble me at all. It has its own charm. I have a job for you, *mademoiselle*. When your aunt leaves I would be very pleased if you would stay here in France. The job I have for you would be much more profitable and well within your capabilities.'

Downright panic flashed across Lucy's face. The idea of working for Guy Chabrol day in and day out alarmed her more than anything she could think of. He made her feel strange just by being there. She hardly dared look at him unless he had goaded her into rage.

'I don't like you!' she blurted out immediately in a flare of honesty.

'That is of no importance,' he assured her, his dark eyes narrowed. 'Liking or not liking are unimportant in this job.'

'I wouldn't like being anywhere near you,' she persisted anxiously, ready to take to her heels.

'It would only be necessary for a little while.'

'I—I'm sorry, *monsieur*. I'm sure you're being kind,' Lucy gulped worriedly. 'Even so, I don't want to work for you, thank you.'

'It is not exactly work, *mademoiselle*.' He looked at her steadily, his glance moving over her rather frantic face. 'It would assure you a very bright future with no need whatever to be at the beck and call of your aunt, with no need to take any dull job for the rest of your life.'

That seemed to be a happy thought and Lucy looked at him with a mixture of suspicion and uncertainty. Being offered a job was the last thing she had expected, unless he was prepared to pay for the right to goad her?

'How long would it take?' she asked cautiously and he shrugged.

'One year, perhaps eighteen months. It is difficult to say.'

It didn't seem long and she knew almost certainly that her aunt had only brought her to France to be kind. It was charitable but, then again, she didn't like charity. She watched his haughty face for a minute and he seemed quite content to keep silent while she thought about it.

'What sort of work?' she enquired with the same caution, quite ready to say no speedily but a little dismayed when she compared being near this irritating, arrogant man and being back in the dull job she envisaged. She was somehow singingly alive here.

'As I have said, it is not exactly work.' He looked at her steadily. 'I want you to have a child. My child.'

CHAPTER FOUR

FOR a second Lucy was too stunned to react at all and then she felt panic-stricken, shocked and embarrassed all at once. The confusing feelings raced through her and mixed together leaving her speechless and pale, near horror on her face.

'Do not refuse out of hand,' the count rasped as he saw her looks. 'I would of course marry you before this event. Afterwards you would be free to return to England and divorce me. Even so, you would remain the Comtesse de Chauvrais. You would receive an allowance that would make you quite rich and give you independence. Even when you remarried, as the mother of my child the allowance would continue as would the title. I do not intend ever to marry in any serious capacity.'

Lucy didn't answer. She just jumped up and made for the door and safety as quickly as possible. Not quickly enough. He was there before her, his back to the door, his face very implacable.

'Please let me out.' Her voice shook. She was so shocked that she was trembling all over, her heart beating so heavily that she was sure he would actually see it.

'You are behaving in a very wild manner,' he said severely, looking down at her from his great height. 'I have made what I think is a very reasonable suggestion, one that will benefit both of us. The time needed is but a very small part of your life and thereafter you will be completely free. I propose to marry you openly and legitimately for all to see. Only you and I will know the true state of affairs. Later you may simply go, wealthy, titled and free for the rest of your life. I will have an heir and will have no need whatever to marry.'

'It's unthinkable!'

'Obviously it is not. *I* have thought it.'

'Look,' Lucy began carefully, convinced now that she was facing a lunatic, his behaviour explained. 'People don't do things like that.'

'How do you know, *mademoiselle*?' he asked with cold logic. 'They would not broadcast it about any more than we will.'

'People fall in love, get married and——'

'Fall out of love and get divorced,' he finished drily. 'It is the normal course of events as love does not exist and is merely a respectable word to cover desire. To all intents and purposes we will do exactly the same as others do: fall out of love and get divorced.'

'Look!' Lucy began again, her attempts to placate him fading fast. 'You and I dislike each other, and rightly so!'

'What do you mean, *mademoiselle*—"rightly so"? What is so right about it? I do not dislike you. I find your strange ways quite fascinating. During the course of this brief marriage I will be constantly amused by your peculiarities. When you are pregnant I will take steps to see to it that you do not either climb walls or fall over.'

'Have you quite finished?' Lucy seethed, realising now that this had been his way of passing a dull afternoon.

'Not exactly,' he murmured. 'When I kissed you before I did not find you repulsive and that convinced me that you would do very well for a temporary wife. You are fresh and innocent and that is also suitable. I would not like a woman well versed in the ways of men to be the mother of my child.'

'You've missed out one small detail,' Lucy snapped, red-faced but now furious. 'I find *you* repulsive!'

'Let us see,' he mused quietly as he pulled her forward and into his arms.

He was kissing her before she could draw breath and her struggles and panic did nothing to deter him. As she subsided he drew her even closer, his hands expertly coaxing her until she was resting against him with all thought of fight gone, hazy mists and lights swinging through her head, feelings driving away common sense.

'Repulsive?' he enquired wryly as his lips left hers and moved to her neck and her ears. 'With your eyes closed and your lips beneath mine, Lucinda, you forget to be repulsed.'

'I'm not Lucinda,' she managed in a whisper. 'I've always been called Lucy. Only my aunt——'

'It is not a suitable name for a countess,' he whispered back mockingly, his lips close to her ear. 'Think of it! Lucy, Comtesse de Chauvrais. It does not carry enough dignity.'

The quiet sarcasm brought Lucy to her senses rapidly and she struggled free.

'It won't need to! I haven't any dignity either, so obviously the idea is idiotic. Get yourself a dignified woman. What about Madame Gatien? She has the dignity of a cobra!'

'And a matching skin,' he added, grinning down at her, sparks of genuine amusement in his dark eyes. 'I have picked you, Lucinda. This is no spur of the moment idea. I have been toying with it for some time. When I saw you at the hotel in Paris I chose you; that is one of the reasons why your aunt is allowed here.'

'One of the reasons?' Lucy asked quickly, intrigued by his behaviour as she had no intention of it concerning her. 'What are the other reasons?'

'Agree to have my child and I might very well tell you,' he countered quickly, his lips quirking at her speedy change from rage to suspicion. 'The only other way you will find out may perhaps be somewhat painful.'

'I'll have to risk it,' Lucy snapped. 'And now, if you don't mind, I would like to go.'

'Mais certainement, mademoiselle,' he said mockingly. 'I will speak of this again.'

'Whenever you like,' Lucy agreed as she moved to the now open door. 'Just see to it, though, *monsieur*, that you don't speak of it to me.'

Once the door was closed behind her she literally fled to her room. She was now, after several days here, able to find her way to her room with no difficulty, but, in any case, right at this moment she didn't care, just as long as Guy Chabrol couldn't find her.

She sank down at the side of the bed and tried to unscramble her mind. He was mad. He had to be. It must be something about his aristocratic breeding. She would ask her aunt to send her back to England and if necessary she would tell her the whole story.

She gave a shudder when she thought of herself in the count's arms. He made her forget everything. He had made her forget everything when he had kissed her in the stables. The crackle of the fire drew her attention. It was already alight and blazing cheerfully. Had this been one of his tricks to soften her up? No! He was just amusing himself.

The thought made her feel better. She would not mention a word of this to her aunt. By dinnertime he would have found something else to occupy his mind. Maybe he would shoot one of the servants for amusement. It didn't seem at all unlikely with the great daunting château around her, the long dark passages, the sullen faces of the staff.

She locked the door securely and went to get a bath. If her aunt wanted her she would just have to manage. Nothing would get her down those stairs until dinnertime when the count's stepmother would be there too. She was disapproving, annoyed, and barely civil but at least she wasn't stark raving mad!

Dinner merely proved to be an added embarrassment. Lucy waited and waited in her room until she was late and her arrival in the dining-room was less than elegant; in fact she almost skidded in at the very last moment just as they were about to be seated.

It appeared to cause a great deal of aloof surprise in Véronique Chabrol and even more in the butler and maid who were standing by to serve the meal. Her aunt looked at her in surprise and Lucy dared not even meet the eyes of the count—she knew how he would look and what he would say given the chance.

He surprised her.

'Good. You have arrived. I was about to send someone to fetch you, *mademoiselle*.'

He came around and helped her to her seat, smiling down at her with no sign of his caustic humour. Her aunt took over the conversation at once as usual and it only drew more attention to Lucy, a thing she wished to avoid at all costs.

'Where on earth were you this afternoon, Lucinda?' Wanda asked as they all settled down. 'You disappeared for simply hours.'

'Lucinda was with me, *madame*,' the count interposed smoothly before Lucy could even look up. 'You have perhaps forgotten? I did however ask your permission.'

Wanda looked astonished and the countess blinked rapidly at the sound of Lucy's name on her stepson's lips.

'Oh! Of course I remember, *monsieur*. I was a little worried, that's all, because you said for a moment only and she was away for a long time. I assumed that Lucinda had disappeared outside. It worries me.'

'She was with me for some considerable time,' Guy Chabrol assured her. 'Also when she is out of doors I am usually with her. There is no need to worry about her safety.'

It gave her aunt pause for thought, apparently, and it also drew further attention to Lucy's red cheeks. And it wasn't true anyway; she wasn't usually with him outside—she deeply regretted that she had ever seen him outside! Everybody seemed to be staring at her and she couldn't manage even a quick glare at him. It turned out to be a very subdued meal with everyone stealing furtive looks at Lucy, and Guy looking at her steadily for the whole time.

After the meal Lucy escaped and Wanda came to her room.

'Just what exactly is going on between you and the count?' she wanted to know as soon as Lucy had let her in. 'It's perfectly dangerous to be meeting a man like that secretly. You've had very little experience of life, Lucinda, and he's a very sophisticated man. He's not like any of the boys you've known at home.'

'I haven't been meeting the count,' Lucy protested. 'I don't even like him. It's just that——' She didn't get any further. Her aunt's eyes were on the glowing fire.

'He's ordering comforts for you that I haven't got. Do be sensible, Lucinda, dear. My room is like an ice-box. He doesn't intend you to freeze, does he? A man like that doesn't do things for nothing. He's softening you up and I should think it's obvious what for.'

'I complained! That's why I've got the fire. He didn't light it himself,' Lucy said, her cheeks very flushed. If her aunt knew what Guy Chabrol had suggested she would be having hysterics. 'I expect you could have a fire if you said you were cold.'

'I doubt it! In any case, I'm not at all bothered about that. I *am* bothered about you, though. You could be at some risk with that man. I've seen how he watches you and you're so—so unworldly. I've been debating whether or not to send you back to England, actually.'

She couldn't have said anything to please Lucy more.

'Oh, I'd like that very much, if you don't need me,' Lucy told her eagerly, seeing a chance of getting away from here. 'When do you want me to go?'

'The sooner the better, I should think. I'll see what I can come up with. I know you've left your job to come with me but you can easily go back to my house. You could earn your keep. I've been thinking of sacking Mrs Brown. You could look after the house and do the cooking. It's quite expensive to pay a daily help and if you did it there would just be your keep and a bit of spending money. You're a good cook.'

Lucy was suddenly looking at a grey picture of her future life, an unpaid servant to her aunt or a dull as ditchwater job. Guy Chabrol's offer came into her mind and she pulled herself up sharply as she actually found herself considering it. The whole future looked bleak, though.

'I can get a job by myself when I go back,' Lucy warned her aunt firmly.

'For goodness' sake, Lucinda, you're my niece! Whatever do you imagine you could do in any case? You're surely not thinking of going back to that dreary estate agent's? In any case, you have no home now. You know as well as I do that they're pulling the Old Mill down—should have been demolished years ago! No, you can live with me from now on. You can help me, run the house, type up my notes. It's going to be quite cosy. From time to time you can come back to France with me too, but, for now, I've got to get you away from the count!'

Wanda left with a satisfied smile and Lucy felt empty. For years she had managed everything for her mother and father, afraid to leave them in case they made such a muddle of their lives that she would never be able to straighten them out, taking a perfectly miserable job when she would have liked to spread her wings.

If she followed a similar path with her aunt she would end up as a prim old maid. She caught a glimpse of herself in the mirror and hastily looked away. She had never even thought things like that before but now she remembered the excitement that had threatened to submerge her when Guy Chabrol held her and kissed her. She got ready for bed with troubled feelings. She would certainly get some job when she got back to England. She was wasting her life away and she had already wasted enough of it.

She was a trifle grim-faced the next morning, sorting out her aunt's haphazard notes as Wanda left the library muttering that she would not be long. Guy Chabrol walked in almost immediately but she resolutely kept her head down.

'During this day I will need an answer to my suggestion of yesterday,' he said softly, coming to lean against the desk and look down at her. 'Avoiding my eyes is not going to make me change my mind. I am well aware that you are shy unless you are in a small rage. It is something that I can easily cope with.'

She didn't either answer or look up and he came closer, tilting her face and looking into her wide blue eyes.

'You have been thinking about it,' he murmured astutely, his gaze narrowed on her face. 'What is your decision?'

'No,' Lucy whispered and his lips twisted ruefully.

'Then we will have to come at this the hard way, *mademoiselle*,' he informed her quietly. 'It is a pity. I would have spared you if I could. I do not particularly want the mother of my child to be resentful.' He sighed and stroked one long finger down her flushed cheek and Lucy came to agitated life.

'I'm going back to England. My aunt wants me to leave very quickly.'

'Does she?' He was instantly alert, his eyes scanning her flushed face. 'When did she reach this decision?'

'Last night. I haven't told her about... She just wants me to go back and...' He just went on looking at her and she jumped up in agitation. 'There's nothing you can do...'

'We will see,' he mused, looking down at her intently. 'Marry me and I will spare you a lot of grief, a lot of unpleasantness.'

'No!' She was suddenly very scared and it showed on her face but she was also adamant. She wasn't as scared as she would be if she agreed to this unbelievable suggestion, and she was beginning to think he really meant it.

'Very well, Lucinda,' he said softly. 'Just remember later that this could all have been done in a civilised manner.'

'What are you going to do?' She looked up into his determined face. He smiled mockingly.

'I am not going to carry you off and make up your mind for you if that is what is so worrying,' he assured her. 'I need to be legally married, my child the heir to my estate and title with no possibility of dispute. You may let wild thoughts die, *mademoiselle*. Our marriage will be legal and dry as dust.'

'It will also be a figment of your imagination,' Lucy informed him, her nerve somewhat restored.

'I intend it to happen. I have chosen you and I am not about to let the chance slip by and have to begin all over again. I am thirty-four. I lead a very busy life and I do not wish to become a father when I am in my dotage.

My son will have to be trained to inherit everything. I must get this duty over with and then I will be able to live my life as I choose, all responsibility ended.'

'You don't think a baby is a responsibility, then?' she enquired sarcastically. It only had his dark eyes narrowing further.

'Not to me, and not to you either if you agree, because you will be gone. You will be rich and titled with no further worries in your life. My child will have everything in any case,' he added coldly.

'Except love, an emotion you don't believe in,' Lucy cut in. 'Some things can't be bought, *monsieur*.'

'And you are one of them, as I can see. You will change your mind, Lucinda, because I need you and I intend to settle my life, perhaps this very day.'

Lucy had no time to reply, because her aunt walked in, looking anxious when she saw the count with Lucy.

'Ah, *madame*. I have been waiting for you,' he announced. 'I need a certain book but I did not want to take it until I knew for sure that you were not using it for your research.'

'Of course, *monsieur*,' Wanda said uneasily. 'Which one? I'm not using many. It's most unlikely that——'

'The green one,' he said pleasantly. 'The leather-bound green book that your niece was reaching for yesterday. I cannot now see it either on the shelves or on the desk you use. Perhaps you have been reading it in your room?'

'Well, no. I—I . . .' Wanda looked round the room for inspiration but none came and she faced the count's dark eyes with a very flushed face.

'Then where is it, *madame*?' he asked quietly. 'I know it was here yesterday. It is, as you probably know, the most valuable book in this room. It is priceless. Neither of you will be allowed to leave here until the book is found.'

'How—how dare you, *monsieur*?' Wanda demanded angrily, as Lucy looked at him in horror. 'Are you suggesting that Lucinda or I...? What about the servants?'

'I am merely searching for a book, *madame*, and pointing out its value. As to the servants, none are allowed in here except Madame Gatien. She has been with my family for years and is above reproach. The château and its contents are in my keeping. It is my duty to guard them. I therefore require the book. At once, *s'il vous plâit*!'

'If you wish to search my room, *monsieur*...' Wanda said angrily.

'Regrettably, I do, *madame*, unless you can tell me where you put the book. It is distasteful but necessary.'

'I shall leave here at once!'

'When the book is discovered.' It sounded utterly menacing and Lucy was too shocked to be embarrassed. The room was filled with books and he only had to search, so why was he making this scene? Her aunt looked very upset and Lucy was unable to help at all; everything seemed to have gone out of control with frightening speed.

The book was not in Wanda's room, although she turned it upside-down in front of the cold dark eyes of her host. The eyes were then turned on Lucy.

'Your room if you please, *mademoiselle*,' he requested quietly, and Lucy went tight-lipped to her own room, the count and Wanda following. Dread was in her mind as if she had walked into some diabolical trap, and she remembered her fear as she had seen this daunting château, as she had seen this daunting man. Had it been a premonition of all this?

It didn't take much of a search. It was in the bottom of Lucy's case, wrapped carefully and placed in a thick envelope and Lucy just stared at it without a word. She was so stunned that she could think of nothing at all to say.

'Lucinda! How could you?' Wanda's voice was filled with distress. 'I know you've got no money but how could you shame me after all I've done for you?'

Lucy turned dazed eyes on her aunt, her mind unable to struggle out of this nightmare. 'Aunt Wanda, I didn't——' she began, but the count took control at once, his cold gaze on Wanda.

'Mademoiselle Balfour does not speak French,' he pointed out harshly. 'She could not have known the value of this book or what it would fetch with a private collector. Innocence does not sit easily on your face, *madame*. Your niece is merely the method of getting the book out of France should you be suspected. Unfortunately, it means that you are both thieves and the police will have to be called. I would like you to remain in your room until I send for you. Do not attempt to leave the château. You would not get very far and it would merely add to the unpleasantness.'

He turned to Lucy. 'I will speak to you downstairs, *mademoiselle*. Come with me.'

Lucy looked at her aunt and needed no further proof. There was nothing but annoyance now on her face; no remorse, no embarrassment. It was all true. She followed him down the long passages and down the stairs, all rebellion crushed. The only thing in her mind was that her own aunt had done this, had not only taken the book but had arranged for Lucy to shoulder the blame if she should be caught.

Now she understood why, after years of indifference, her aunt had found her company necessary, but still the reality of theft would not sink in. The world seemed to have crashed in on her with brutal force since she had been here.

The idea of police filled her with dread. They would say that she was an accomplice. Guy Chabrol had already said as much and he clearly believed it. Her only chance was to plead with him and she knew how far that would get her. He was cold and dominant, icily cold now as he walked beside her across the darkened hall.

'Sit down,' he ordered as she went with him to the small room he had used the previous day, but she could hardly move from the doorway. He closed the door and indicated the chair she had sat in before.

'I'll stand, thank you,' she whispered but he came and took her firmly by the arm, leading her to the chair.

'You will sit,' he grated and she didn't seem to have much choice.

'I didn't take that book,' Lucy said, looking up at him white-faced. 'I saw it for the first time yesterday when I nearly fell from the ladder. I've not seen it since until——'

'Your aunt took the book,' he assured her grimly. 'It is not the first time that she has stolen books. The last two stolen were, however, from people I know, and she was out of France before their loss was discovered. It was then too late and pointless to accuse her. No doubt she has done it many times before but the owners have kept quiet or not yet discovered their loss.'

'So—so why did you let her come here?' She was bewildered, unable to look away from the cold eyes that watched her relentlessly.

'I intended to catch her. The last time she stole a book of value it was taken from a very old man, a man I have known all my life. For him, living in a château does not denote wealth. If his books were to have been sold he could well have used the money himself, but instead he held on to them, the history of his family, treasures handed to him for safekeeping as mine were handed to me. He has never fully recovered from the loss, from the shock of knowing that a woman who was granted the privilege of seeing and using such treasures should then rob him. I assumed that I would be on her list. I made myself readily available.'

She could understand now how he had walked into her aunt's blundering trap. His trap had had a great deal more finesse, and she was in it herself.

'You—you might not have caught her,' Lucy ventured in a low voice, seeing again the ruthless power on his face.

'There is an inventory. Had I missed her sleight of hand you would not have been given transport from here until I had checked that inventory. In any case, I had a very good idea of the book she would select. It was the most valuable, the one most likely to interest a collector. It would have disappeared for all time, for some greedy person to gloat over in secret. It was given to one of my ancestors by the king himself and it is of great interest to more than my family. Students have the use of this library from time to time. It is visited by students from all over the world.'

'Then my aunt must have known that...'

'She knew,' he assured her grimly. 'Her books may be scantily researched but her victims are researched thoroughly. But she did not know quite everything.' He looked at her steadily, his dark eyes like stone. 'There is indeed talent in your family, Mademoiselle Balfour. Your mother was an artist, your father a poet and your aunt is a thief.'

'But I'm not!' Lucy pleaded urgently.

'Indeed? How will you prove it to the police, *mademoiselle*? It is obvious from her reaction that she will not exonerate you. The best you can hope for is that she will take the major blame and that you will be classed as merely an accomplice. You will probably get a lesser sentence.'

Lucy's face went whiter than ever. In her mind, cell doors were already closing on her and the count looked implacable.

'You know I didn't take it,' she whispered, her eyes blue and enormous.

'Yes, I know,' he agreed calmly. 'I have already said that you are as clear as glass, utterly without subtlety. When I saw you in Paris I must admit I imagined you to be an accomplice but after only a few words with you I decided that you could not possibly be dishonest. Innocence is clearly on your face as guilt is on your aunt's face.'

'Then you can tell the police that . . .'

'I am merely telling you, *mademoiselle*,' he pointed out. 'I am setting your mind at rest. This conversation will go no further. The police will draw their own conclusions and there is little doubt as to what those conclusions will be. Even I may be wrong; perhaps you are cleverer than you look?'

'How can you do this?' Lucy gasped, staring at his implacable face in horror.

'I need an heir and I have no desire to be married permanently. I do not trust women at all. I have chosen you to be my wife for a little while, the mother of my child. I did inform you that the way there may well be painful as you refused to agree. You now have two choices. Marry me or go to prison with your aunt. The book is more valuable than you imagine. The sentence may well be lengthy.'

'You're a maniac,' she whispered, looking up at him with shocked eyes, a wave of faintness washing over her.

'But a very determined one,' he assured her. 'The choice is yours, *mademoiselle*, and you have about two minutes to make that choice. I cannot delay my call to the police for much longer.'

'My aunt will tell them that——'

'If you agree, it is my intention to set your aunt free and send her on her way,' he murmured in what he appeared to think was a reasonable tone. 'You will remain here with me and she will be under no illusions as to what will happen to her should she ever return to France. In any case, it would be pointless. I will circulate her name. You have the ability to allow her to go free and escape a term in prison, you also have the ability to escape from the shame yourself. The decision is yours alone.'

'I haven't done anything at all,' Lucy whispered. 'It's not fair.'

'C'est la vie, mademoiselle,' he murmured sardonically. 'There are winners and there are losers. You have lost.'

'I—I couldn't bear to be in prison,' Lucy pleaded. 'I can't bear to be trapped indoors, even.'

'Marry me, Lucinda, and you will have a lifetime of freedom. At the very most you will be needed for eighteen months. After that you will be rich, titled and free, with the total freedom that comes from wealth without responsibility, and you will have earned it.'

'I don't have a choice, do I?' she asked weakly, but he smiled, his brows raised ironically.

'Most certainly you do, Lucinda. The choice is simple. My wife for a little time or prison for a long time. Make your choice now!'

'All right,' she whispered, her eyes downcast, her mind still trying to refuse to believe it.

'Louder, *mademoiselle*. I wish you to make no mistake about this. You will be unable to take back any promise, because I will not hesitate to have your aunt brought back to France and to accuse you both. Therefore say it louder so that you will remember.'

'All right!' Lucy shouted, standing up with clenched hands to face this tormentor. It was the final thing to make her shock resurface and the world swayed dizzily as she collapsed back into the chair, her eyes closed and her face as white as chalk.

When she came round a second later he was kneeling by her, a glass of brandy in his hand, some even now being trickled between her pallid lips, and she looked at him accusingly.

'I'll always hate you,' she said in a low, trembling voice.

'Hate, Lucinda?' he queried wryly. 'You are not made for hatred. If you had been then it would have been directed at life long ago and you would not have sublimated your life for others. You would not even know how to begin to hate.'

He stroked back the soft hair from her forehead, his hand lingering on her skin.

'I am not a savage. While you are with me you may have anything you want. Perhaps when you go we will even remain friends, eh?'

She couldn't stop the shudder that ran over her skin. If she had to choose a friend it would never be anyone who forced her into marriage with prison as the alternative. It would not in any case be someone like Guy Chabrol. Power radiated from him, power and ruthlessness. He was outside her understanding.

He came to escort Lucy down to dinner and it was as well that he did. She was so filled with shock and the feeling of unreality that she would never have managed alone. So far she had not one idea about how to get herself out of this but she knew that she must. There had been a terrible scene with her aunt, and only Guy's fury and cold threats had stopped her vicious tongue as she had turned on Lucy.

Now he was cold and calm, waiting for her.

'Nobody at all knows of this except you and I,' he informed her as he waited at her door and watched her reluctance to move from her room, observed her pale face and her uneasiness. 'There is no need whatever for anyone, not even Véronique, to be enlightened. The matter is closed and you are simply about to become my wife.'

Lucy was grateful, astonishingly so when she thought of the price she would have to pay for this consideration. It was Guy Chabrol who had got her into it, after all. Not entirely, she mused. Aunt Wanda had set her up with no mercy whatever and she knew that if she had gone to England as her aunt had suggested there would have been no mercy there either. She would have been offered a trip to France each time her aunt wished to steal another book.

He simply announced his plans with no preamble. When they were seated at the table, Véronique looking surprised but relieved that Wanda was not there, Guy made his announcement.

'Madame Balfour has left the château,' he stated calmly. 'She had a pressing need to return to England and will not be coming back to France.'

'I hope it's not a serious matter, *mademoiselle*?' Véronique said politely, looking intrigued that Lucy was still there but too courteous to ask why.

'It could have become serious had she remained,' Guy murmured blandly. 'Trouble has been averted, though. Lucinda is to remain, however. She has consented to be my wife.'

It was a bombshell of some proportion, its effect stunning. Véronique Chabrol simply stared, apparently speechless, and there was a great rattle of silver as the butler juggled with a tray that seemed to have been about to fall from his nerveless fingers.

'It—it is so sudden,' Véronique muttered with difficulty. 'I had no idea that...'

'Things like this are very often sudden,' Guy murmured smoothly, glancing at Lucy with a smile that must have cost him a lot. It was almost loving. 'When the time came, I could not bear to let her go. Had she gone, I would merely have followed her and what is the sense in that? We know our own minds already. I have seen more of Lucinda than anyone realises. We plan to marry very speedily.'

During the rest of the meal Lucy was very conscious of Véronique's eyes on her. She was being summed up for her new position and definitely being found wanting. It made her more nervous and gauche than ever. It was only with Guy Chabrol that she seemed to realise her own character. The very man who had scared her from the first sight of him and who had now trapped her was the only one who appeared to be able to bring her out of her shell.

Mostly it was anger that did it but she had never felt anger like that with anyone before. He also made her feel very safe sometimes and she cast a sidelong glance at him as he sat dark and powerful at the head of the table. She didn't know him at all. How could she go through with it? Her mind refused to contemplate the details. She must get away.

Later, Lucy found herself alone with the count once more as he invited her to take coffee with him and she blurted out her fears without much thought.

'I'm not suitable for this job! I'm not going to fit in with your lifestyle for even a day. Your stepmother already knows it. Even the servants glare at me and——'

'They are not glaring at you,' he informed her in amusement, 'they are simply glaring. They do not like being here. It is as alien to them as it is to you. My family have not lived here for generations. This place is never used. There is a caretaker, several in fact, and they are now taking a short break. The butler was called out of retirement to impress your aunt. Tomorrow he will return with considerable joy to his own house, the staff will be back on duty and we will return to my house closer to Paris. Nobody lives here, Lucinda. It is normally only opened when students wish to use the library. They make their appointments through their colleges and——'

'Then, why...?'

'A honeyed trap to catch a thief,' he explained drily. 'That it also caught you is very satisfying but originally it was merely intended to catch your aunt. In the normal course of events you would have found the château apparently deserted. In any case, it is well out of the way and not in the guidebooks. I did not plan this on the spur of the moment. The wrath of the servants is quite understandable. They think, like you, that I have taken leave of my senses. Tomorrow you will see a great improvement in their general attitude. I have ordered that the place be closed again and the following week it will be back as it was originally, the caretaking staff here, no sign that anyone has lived here for centuries. Your aunt was well aware of the value of my library but she did not know that we rarely even visit this dismal place.'

'You were prepared to go to all this trouble to get my aunt?' Lucy looked at him with some awe.

'I am prepared to take trouble with any scheme I have.'

He looked at her evenly and her face flooded with colour. She felt almost sick with apprehension.

'I can't... How will I be able to...? Babies don't just appear!' she stammered, her face even more red when he smiled mockingly.

'Let us leave that matter in abeyance for now. There are several hurdles to cross before then, not least a marriage for which you will have to be prepared. We will get to know each other. I have already told you that I am not a barbarian.'

Oh, but he was! It was cold-blooded, terrifying. She wanted to set off running and never stop until she was safe. He had said that he would fetch them back, though, and such was her awe of his power that she believed he would be able to do that. She would never get out of France.

'I'm trapped,' she whispered and the dark eyes narrowed on her distressed face.

'It is a golden trap though, *mademoiselle*,' he assured her. 'I intend to be kind to you. Do not make that promise impossible to keep. There will be no need to fight me.'

'I'm not suitable... Why did you choose me?' Lucy asked tremulously.

He leaned back in his seat and looked at her coolly.

'My choices were limited, *mademoiselle*. There are many women who would have been willing to become the Comtesse de Chauvrais but they would be world-wise, greedy, determined to cling to the reality of their position here in France. You are innocent and fresh, very anxious to leave. I do not want a woman clinging to me; they have clung before and showed their faithlessness later. My life is my own. It is my intention to remain free. You are most suitable. All you require is a few days of instruction and a little more poise.'

'You can't give me enough poise to be a countess,' Lucy said desperately, hoping he would even now change his mind. He was not about to do so.

'Poise will only be required in social gatherings and they will be few. At other times you may be yourself. You amuse me as you are. It will pass the time more quickly.'

'What you need is a clown!' Lucy said heatedly, desperation giving her courage.

'I need you and I have you,' he assured her harshly. 'Go to bed. Tomorrow we go home.'

'I haven't got a home.' She looked at him stubbornly and he frowned alarmingly.

'You have a home with me until my child is old enough to be left,' he grated.

'You haven't got a child, *monsieur*,' Lucy said with some satisfaction, her head tilted proudly, her mind wriggling about trying to come up with a suitable plan of escape.

'Not yet,' he agreed. 'But that is the point of the exercise, is it not, *mademoiselle*? If I did not need an heir, I would not need you. You would be in a police car at this moment with your aunt. When you are thinking resentfully of me, remember that without her I would not have been able to capture you. Consider the two crimes and decide which of us is the more guilty of cruelty.'

'You're both as bad!' Lucy muttered, her moment of pride shattered.

'Tell me that in two years' time,' he murmured as he led her to the door. 'My château near Paris is warm and comfortable, surrounded by gardens. Accept things gracefully and you will be happy.'

'I'm going to hate you!' Lucy threatened as she went off up the dark stairs. He said nothing at all and when she glanced back he was still watching her, his dark eyes brooding and still, fathomless and cold. Nothing would make him change his mind, she knew that. She had to make some plan of her own. To really agree to his plan was unthinkable.

CHAPTER FIVE

IN SPITE of a near-sleepless night Lucy had no plan next morning. It was as if she was being swept up into something she had no control of at all. They left the château, some of the staff leaving too and others remaining to remove all signs of their occupancy.

The servants were now much more normal-looking, all except Madame Gatien who appeared to have been born with an icy expression that was never to leave her face. The smiles in Lucy's direction from the other servants surprised her until Guy drily pointed out the reason.

'They are now content that their discomfort has been worth while since it has given me a romantic interlude with my future wife,' he informed Lucy in a taunting voice. 'They feel part of the liaison.'

Lucy looked hastily away. 'Do you normally keep them abreast of your affairs?'

'News travels fast in the servants' quarters. I announced my intentions in front of those serving dinner. It removed the necessity of a more formal introduction. They now know you are to be the new Comtesse de Chauvrais. You will be treated accordingly.'

They were alone in the car, travelling swiftly towards Paris. Véronique had left the night before, unable, it seemed, to bear even one more night in the Château de Rochaine, and Lucy would not have wanted her there. Since Guy's sudden announcement, Véronique had been looking at her with concern and Lucy knew why. She would never be suitable; the looks said everything.

Madame Gatien was of the same opinion if her looks were to be believed.

'You know that this is all ridiculous and that I won't be able to cope, don't you?' She gave a small sigh, her head turned firmly to the window and away from the count.

'You know the consequences of trying to back out of this deal,' he rasped, the quiet mockery leaving him instantly.

'I'm not trying to back out,' Lucy informed him tightly. 'I know I'm trapped. What I'm saying is that I won't be able to cope.'

'Necessity is the mother of invention. You will manage because you must. In any case, I will be there, right beside you.'

'Is that supposed to calm me?' Lucy enquired angrily, turning on him. 'It's the most threatening thing I can think of.'

'I can think of prison. That sounds much more threatening to me.' He was silent for a long time and then he glanced at her in exasperation. 'Stop fighting me, Lucinda. You will come out of this very well and I need you. I need you enough to be very generous.'

'You've bought me, you mean?' Lucy muttered bitterly. He flared into rage, stopped the car and glared at her furiously.

'No! I have trapped you, captured you and I have done it very easily. The wealth and the title will be yours when you have produced my child, *then* I will have bought you! The way you behave leads me to believe that I will have paid very dearly for you. Did I not dislike your aunt so roundly, I would sympathise with her. You should have been beaten, perhaps, when you were a child. Maybe I will beat you!'

'I'd like to see you try!' Lucy turned on him with eyes like saucers, sparks flashing from the deep blue. He glared at her for a second longer and then began to laugh quietly, his face lighting up with amusement.

'This child of ours will take some controlling. You have a temper to match my own.' He suddenly pulled her forward and kissed her roughly on the mouth. 'You little shrew,' he murmured against her lips.

She pulled frantically away and he let her go, straightening up and starting the car again.

'Don't *kiss* me!' she said in a small furious voice, rising panic at the back of it, but his laughter was still there.

'I will only kiss you when it is necessary,' he assured her with a glittering sidelong glance at her flushed face. 'At that moment the servants passed in the estate car. They will now be assuring themselves that their discomfort was all worth while. The French, *ma chère*, are a very romantic race. There is another estate car not too far behind with the rest of the staff in it. Annoy me further and I will give them also the delight of a demonstration of affection.'

Lucy huddled into her corner and it seemed to give him a great deal of sardonic satisfaction. He glanced at her tightly clenched hands and his low laughter shivered right through her body.

'Even someone as prim and old-fashioned as you must realise that some sort of physical contact will be necessary eventually.'

Lucy didn't know whether he was trying to embarrass her or be carefully sensible. It was as well to imagine the worst with Guy Chabrol.

'I don't want to talk about it,' she said tightly. It wasn't going to happen anyway. The closer to Paris the better she would feel. Escape would be at hand.

'You prefer to keep your mind comfortably blank? It is unwise. It would be better to grow accustomed to being held and kissed.'

'In case the shock kills me?' Lucy retorted, her face turned firmly away. 'I'm quite sure you like this no better than I do so let's not pretend, *monsieur*.'

'Guy,' he corrected firmly. 'You cannot go on calling your future husband *monsieur*. It will astonish Véronique. As to my feelings, I have explained that it is necessity. However, I do not mind kissing you. I do not find you repulsive, as I have pointed out. Accept things calmly.'

'Maybe I can be hypnotised!' Lucy snapped, moving uncomfortably in her seat. 'I'll give it some thought. Meanwhile, *monsieur*, I would like it very much if you either changed the subject or kept silent.'

'Very well.' He sighed wearily. 'You are not making things easy, Lucinda.'

'You've not made things easy for me!'

'I have tried,' he assured her quietly.

He took her advice and kept silent and Lucy turned away, biting her lip and asking herself who was really to blame for this state of affairs. Wanda's name came immediately to her mind. It was her aunt who had got her into this predicament. Even that wasn't strictly true. If she hadn't jumped at the chance to leave her job she would never have been anywhere near France, would never have even met Guy Chabrol.

She felt a small twinge of unease as she realised that she would not have liked that at all. He was the most exciting thing that had ever happened to her in her whole life. She was more alive than she had ever been. If only he could have been normal!

She sighed, her shoulders falling from their tense stance and he glanced across at her.

'*Pauvre petite,*' he murmured softly. 'I am sorry that you find yourself in this trap. I cannot release you, because you are perfect, necessary for my plans. I will be kind. Do not fear the future so much.'

'I'm not afraid,' Lucy said coldly. 'I'm just thinking my own thoughts.'

'See that they do not run to escape,' he murmured darkly. 'Try that and you *will* have cause for fear!'

Lucy turned her head away to hide her eyes, but her mind still saw him and her lips still felt his kisses. It was all impossible, mad!

With Paris not yet in sight Guy turned the car off the motorway and headed across country. So his house near Paris was a country house? Providing that it was not as forbidding as the country of the Château de Rochaine it would be better than any bright lights for Lucy. She cheered up and looked out at the trees. She would be able to cope much better in a normal house, until she could get away.

Guy seemed to be quite content to drive and say nothing at all and Lucy gave all her attention to the village they reached. It stretched along the road sleepily, a few shops, a few houses with small gardens and nothing more. It looked reasonably boring, perfectly safe.

He turned in at huge gates and the thought of safety vanished as she recognised the crest that had been all too obvious at the forbidding Château de Rochaine.

His glance flashed to her as she gasped in dismay.

'It is not like the Château de Rochaine,' he snapped. 'You will find a great deal of comfort here—and warmth. The whole place is extremely modern.'

Not if the colossal gates were anything to go by, Lucy thought. Her lips tightened at the thought but she couldn't keep them closed. As the 'house' came into sight she just stared and gasped again. It was another château and not on any cosy scale either.

She began to count the windows at the front in an almost hysterical manner. There were thirty-two if you counted the ten nestling against the roof. It was white stone, quite beautiful, almost serene-looking. The front was heavily decorated with what appeared to be gold plaques but she couldn't quite make them out as they approached.

She could see the wide front door standing open, though, and she dreaded going inside, a burning desire in her to refuse to get out of the car.

'Not at all forbidding.' Guy seemed to be greatly pleased with himself and obviously glad to be back. 'It is, as I said, a very comfortable house.'

'It's a great museum of a place!' Lucy snapped. 'Just take a good close look at me, *monsieur*! How do you think I can even begin to cope in such a place? What sort of Comtesse de Chauvrais do you imagine I'll make?'

'I will turn you into a countess!' He stopped the car and glared down at her. 'You will call me Guy and not *monsieur*. We are to be married very soon. As to your appearance, I informed you some time ago that with a visit to the beauty salon and a few expensive clothes you will pass for the real thing—at least, you will manage to do it for the short time that is necessary.'

'Of course I won't!'

Lucy looked at him scornfully, too annoyed to be scared for the moment, and he frowned down at her with a great deal of black annoyance.

'As you have no choice, you will manage perfectly well,' he assured her harshly. 'My plans are made and they include you. Your only alternative is prison—comfortably beside your aunt!'

He was not about to relent and Lucy looked away, back at the house. Since he had trapped her she had not really believed the whole thing deeply. This sort of melodrama didn't happen to people except in films. Her sensible mind had assured her of that and she had felt she was just playing along, almost humouring him as if he were some sort of lunatic.

'I've done nothing at all to deserve this,' she reminded him quietly. 'I'm sure that deep down you don't mean it to happen. I just can't face it, any of it. Please, let me go, and I'll simply disappear out of your life altogether. I'll not even think of contacting my aunt. I'll keep quiet and just—just go home.'

'What home?' he enquired coldly. 'You have no home. The only thing you most assuredly possess is a criminal relative. I would be willing to guess that you do not even have with you the price of the rail fare into Paris, not to speak of the cost of the flight to England from there. Whether you do or not, however, I have decided what your future will be and you have agreed. You will not be allowed to slide out of that agreement. All this is very important to me. You will finally leave France with a title and considerable wealth. As far as I can see it is a very honourable job and one that will benefit both of us.'

'It—it's degrading!' Lucy said miserably, her face pale.

'*Dieu!* Will you stop suggesting that?' he grated. 'It is an arranged marriage and nothing out of the ordinary even in this day and age. The only extraordinary thing is you and your childish attitude. I do not wish to speak of this again, *mademoiselle*!'

'Are you going to go on calling me *mademoiselle* while I call you Guy?' Lucy asked waspishly, suddenly wanting to lash out at him. His brow darkened even further.

'If my plans were not so well made and if I had not already announced our marriage I would fly you to England myself and turn you loose!' he bit out furiously. 'It is quite clear that you have no intention of submitting to this with even one ounce of dignity. You intend to pester and complain throughout our association like a spoiled child!'

'Quite right. I do!' Lucy snapped. 'I intend to kick up a fuss from beginning to end of this ridiculous affair.

I'm not at all sure that it's not criminal either. It seems to me that I'm being blackmailed. You, *Monsieur le Comte*, are a scoundrel and I'll fight every inch of the way, so don't talk to me about submitting with dignity. I won't submit at all and you can't make me!'

She tossed her head defiantly and met astonished dark eyes. For a second he stared at her as if she had taken leave of her senses and then, to her annoyance, his eyes began to laugh. They were laughing long before the amusement touched those long, mobile lips.

'Perhaps I will enjoy that better than if you continue to be a rather boring mouse-like creature,' he mused. 'As to not submitting—we will see, Lucinda.'

'My name is Lucy and I'll not answer if you——'

He jerked her forward and into his arms, his lips covering hers relentlessly, his strong hands subduing her struggles and she collapsed against him, breathless and tingling with shock, plucking feebly at his sleeve until she allowed the harsh warmth to envelope her and subsided into a sort of peace, her mouth willingly turned to his. He kissed her until there were stars swinging in front of her closed eyes.

'Now will you be silent, little wretch?' he murmured as he lifted his head. 'It is not unpleasant to kiss you and it seems to be the only way I can either silence you or bring you to your senses.' He sat her up and started the car, completing the trip to the wide front doors, and Lucy folded her hands in her lap to stop them from trembling visibly, her soft lips set in a stubborn line even though she was burning up inside.

His amused glance slid over her as they stopped at the door.

'Flushed and bewildered,' he commented. 'Good. It is what the servants expect to see. They are much more astute than Véronique; she simply believes everything I tell her.'

'Then she must be constantly deceived,' Lucy snapped. 'I'll see to it that she's kept up to date with things in future.'

'Splendid! Spoken like a countess,' he taunted. 'You will soon be in charge here and quite resigned to your fate.'

No way, Lucy thought bitterly and, as the first face she saw as they stepped inside was that of Madame Gatien, she had no doubts at all.

The château did not take as much getting used to as the Château de Rochaine. Within the first day Lucy was very well orientated and spent some considerable time wandering around alone. With her safely captured Guy seemed to have reverted to his normal attitude of total lack of interest and she was sure Véronique suspected that this was no extraordinary love-match. In fact, she was at great pains to avoid Véronique altogether in case the feelings she had showed on her face, for her mind was still plotting escape.

The gardens that fronted the château were formal and neat, long walks between well-clipped trees, small pools and orderly arrangements of flowers, but the back of the château was a delight. Here there was a small lake, partly overhung with trees and bushes, water-lilies at the edge and tall bulrushes making a secret trail along the south side nearest to the house. She lingered there the next day, her mind avoiding any thought of the future. The tight atmosphere of the previous evening had been more than enough.

About to go back indoors, she stopped when she heard voices from the open window of the room that was Guy's study.

'What exactly do you intend to do about Lucinda?'

Véronique's voice was quite sharp. Obviously she had bearded Guy in his den—no mean task—no act for the faint-hearted.

'I intend to marry her with some speed.' His voice dismissed the query impatiently.

'Guy! She is not... I mean when you take a close look at her... Guy, she will not be suitable as she is. You must do something, take her in hand, alter her appearance. She is not in any way prepared. You must give her at least some resemblance of gloss—of chic.'

'Je ne suis pas un sorcier!'

Guy's impatient growl had Lucy's cheeks flooding with colour. She could follow that all right. He wasn't a wizard and obviously he thought it would take a deal of magic to turn her into anything acceptable.

'Guy!' Véronique sounded shocked. 'If you love this girl then surely you don't want her to be embarrassed when she sees the sort of people you mix with? You must do something to help her!'

'What, exactly?' Lucy heard him push his chair back and begin to pace about. 'She will not in any case be mixing with people a great deal.'

'You intend to simply keep her to yourself and not allow anyone else to see her? There is the wedding. There will have to be dinners to introduce her. Unless you intend to sneak away and——'

'I am not given to sneaking!' Guy was annoyed but Lucy begged to differ. He had, after all, sneaked up on her. '*You* had better do something about her appearance,' he muttered crossly. 'I agree that at the moment she looks very much like a farm servant.'

'*Guy!* Really! I begin to feel sorry for the child. I can well understand why you have not yet married! I certainly will take her in hand. As a lover you closely resemble a dissatisfied commanding officer!'

'Did I say that I was dissatisfied?' he queried drily. 'Lucinda is exactly the wife I want. She will do very well.'

'You sound as if you have sent for her out of the paper—as if she has been purchased! If this is modern love then I am content to be middle-aged!'

Véronique stormed out and went so far as to slam the door, and Lucy felt like storming in. So this was what he thought in that arrogant mind? She was like a farm servant, but she would do nicely for the Comte de Chauvrais for a little while. She wondered what Véronique would say if she knew the whole story.

She didn't storm in though. She went to her room and had a good look at herself, her conclusions no different than they had been before. She looked like a mouse, a cross one at the moment, with resentful, deep blue eyes. No amount of effort from Véronique was going to change that.

She was rather grim-faced at dinner and Guy noticed.

'You are feeling unwell, *ma chère*?' He looked across at her solicitously for the benefit of Véronique and Lucy had a great desire to snap at him. Instead she kept her head lowered.

'I'm perfectly fine, thank you,' she murmured, well aware that Véronique's eyes were on her intently. 'Everything is rather new and strange, though. I'll have to try to get used to it.'

'You will, Lucinda,' Véronique said with angry determination. 'Tomorrow we will go into Paris and—er—fit you out.'

Like a battleship? Lucy cast a small malevolent glance at Guy from beneath her lashes but he was watching closely too and his dark brows rose in surprise that she had the temerity. He took her to task when they were alone after dinner.

'If you continue to throw such looks in my direction then nobody will long be in doubt as to the true state of affairs!' he remonstrated sharply, and Lucy turned on him at once.

'Looks are not what I would like to throw in your direction, *Monsieur le Comte*!' she snapped. 'I would like something much more substantial—like an anvil! And don't you *"ma chère"* me! I'm nothing to you. I just work for you and I'm to be paid when it's all over!'

'*Mon Dieu*, you are a shrew with sharp teeth!' he grated, grasping her arms and pulling her forward. 'If I do not utter some endearment then Véronique will become suspicious!'

He glared down at her and Lucy glared back. 'Isn't she suspicious already? Doesn't she think it odd that you're about to marry someone who looks like a farm servant?'

His face went perfectly still and Lucy blushed brightly at giving away the fact that she had been eavesdropping.

'So! You have been climbing walls again?' he queried softly, his dark eyes narrowed on her flushed face. 'You have been hanging from windowsills and flicking up your little pointed ears?'

'They're *not* pointed!' Lucy raged, embarrassment gone.

He brought her hard against his chest, his eyes staring into hers. 'I will investigate,' he murmured sarcastically, and, before she could move, his teeth had captured her ear, nipping sharply, making her freeze to the spot in case he closed those perfect white teeth on her tender skin.

'Afraid, little mouse?' he murmured, laughter now at the back of his voice. 'Would I injure the one who is to be the new Comtesse de Chauvrais? Relax. It is, after all, love-play.'

His tongue inspected the delicate whorl of her ear and she shuddered, unable to escape when he drew her forward.

'I have told you to relax,' he reminded her softly. 'I am accustomed to being obeyed. I will have to train you.'

He lifted her face, cupping her head in two hands, and kissed her, and Lucy stopped struggling as heat spread from her chest and seemed to reach every part of her body at once. Guy made a peculiar low sound in his throat and drew her fully into his arms as he deepened the kiss, searching her mouth with something like hunger. She forgot everything—forgot why she was there and who she was and when he lifted his head she just stared up at him in a daze.

He didn't look the same. His mocking humour had quite gone and he stared back at her, a frown on his dark face.

'Tomorrow I will accompany you on this shopping trip,' he said abruptly, letting her go and turning away. 'I could do with some light entertainment.'

'Why are you so cruel?' Lucy whispered shakily.

He had entranced her unexpectedly, reducing her to a trembling being in his arms, and now he was back to being sardonic, quite sure that an afternoon with her, watching Véronique attempt to transform her, would be light entertainment.

'I am not cruel,' he muttered harshly, his back to her as he stared out of the window. 'I merely have a greatly developed sense of self-preservation.'

Lucy turned and walked out of the room without answering. It seemed to her the only dignified thing to do. She wished *she* had a greatly developed sense of self-preservation but clearly she hadn't. Guy could get to her without even trying. In any case, she didn't understand him. Her mind told her that she didn't want to anyway but inside she was still quivering, a feeling beginning to

surface that frightened her more than anything she had
ever known. She suddenly felt a bitter sense of loss and
she hugged her arms around herself. If she began to think
with anything but dislike about Guy Chabrol she would
be lost forever.

In her room she too stared out of the window. To say
that she was out of her depth was an understatement of
considerable proportions. She had lived a strange but
very simple life and the château itself told her that her
life here, even though it was for a very short time, would
be beyond her imagining. There was the bargain too.
She faced it squarely for the first time.

She had never even been kissed so possessively as Guy
kissed her. How could she contemplate any real physical
intimacy without love? She would play along with this
temporarily until she could escape. Her mind refused to
see any further into the future. As to having a child and
then willingly leaving it! Real horror enveloped her. She
couldn't think about that.

For the moment there was no way out of this, but it
would come. For now it was too soon. He could still
call the police and, apart from her own horror of it, she
had a foolish lingering desire to see her aunt escape. He
was determined and he could be very cruel—he *was* very
cruel otherwise he would not have trapped her here. He
knew she had no part in her aunt's crimes. He didn't
know what was in her head, though. He just thought he
could take her life into his hard hands and mould it to
his will.

She got ready for bed in a sort of daze, shivering when
she heard Guy come upstairs and walk along to his room.
For a second he stopped outside her door as if he was
thinking of coming in. She was glad the light was out
until she suddenly remembered that he had not looked
too pleased after he had kissed her this evening. Maybe

he had changed his mind? Maybe he was thinking of coming in and telling her she could go?

She reached her hand out to switch on the light but he was already walking away and she sank back to the pillows, her face flushed when she realised that she didn't really want him to send her away. She would never forget him. Perhaps she was lost already? It was not a good thought to take with her into dreams, and in any case her dreams recently had been of Guy's dark, impatient face. She was dreading tomorrow. He was sure to goad with his usual lack of mercy.

CHAPTER SIX

MORNING found Lucy driving to Paris with two slightly hostile companions. Guy was grim and silent and Véronique simply stared out of the window until the city was in sight. Evidently she had not forgiven Guy for his comments to her when she was in his study and also Guy had clearly been dwelling on the subject of Lucy's suitability.

'I will drop you off and join you later for lunch,' he remarked over his shoulder as they entered the city. 'A visit to a beauty salon does not fill me with wild anticipation.'

'As you wish,' Véronique agreed stiffly. 'Perhaps after lunch you will care to take over yourself? After all, I presume you know what you like to see?'

'I might just do that,' Guy countered, with a slanting look at Lucy that promised mischief. She hadn't the faintest idea what they were talking about and felt she would rather not know. The goading look was back in his eyes.

She soon forgot about him as Véronique led her to a glittering beauty salon and issued swift orders with no smile at all. Whether she was ashamed to have to take responsibility for this un-chic English girl, or whether she was still annoyed with Guy, Lucy did not know. She didn't much care, either, after a few minutes because she began to receive the cosseting of a lifetime.

Never before had she done more than wash and brush her hair. Her face had joined the rest of her body in the shower and that had been that. Now she was walked around, fussed over, discussed and worked on by experts.

'A little styling, I think, *madame*.' A very impressive young man walked around Lucy and then addressed himself to the matter of her hair. 'The face is unusual, the large eyes, the high cheekbones. She has the gamine look, yes?'

Véronique nodded impatiently and it was all out of Lucy's hands.

He wielded his scissors with a great deal of flourish and her hair seemed to spring into startled life, pretty much how she felt when Guy touched her. It was curved around her face, widening her cheekbones, enlarging her eyes even more. She watched in astonishment and the young man smirked to himself. He was in no doubt about his skill and her expression bolstered up an already soaring ego.

She was then handed over to the beautician who worked on her face for what seemed like hours. Lucy found herself falling asleep in the comfortable chair, disappointed when she was told to get up.

She gulped as a mirror was held in front of her. The mouse had gone. Except for the clothes, the mouse might never have been there at all. Wide-eyed, clear-skinned, subtly made-up, she hardly recognised herself and she saw a certain amount of grim satisfaction on Véronique's face. It seemed to be some sort of contest between Guy and his stepmother and Véronique was in no doubt that she had won.

When they met Guy for lunch he said nothing at all. He glanced at her very comprehensively but then got on with ordering. Lucy was almost tearfully disappointed. She wanted him to notice how changed she was. She wanted him to be stunned. He wasn't. He simply looked bored. He managed to surprise her though.

'I will take Lucinda with me now,' he stated as lunch finished. 'As you said, I know what I like. I will see to it that she is well on the way to being fitted out before we go home.'

There it was again, the battleship syndrome! Lucy shot a snapping look at him and once again the dark eyebrows rose in astonished enquiry.

'You do not wish to have beautiful clothes?' he asked icily, as they left Véronique and walked back to the busy streets.

'I don't like to be spoken of as if I were a boat that needed a lick of paint!' Lucy snapped.

She had his whole-hearted, amused attention at once.

'The lick of paint has already been applied, most skilfully,' he murmured, glancing over her flushed face. 'They are good, eh?'

'They must be if they've done anything for me.'

She turned her face away but he stopped and tilted it to his, ignoring intrigued passers-by.

'They have brought out the gamine look but it was already there. Do not underestimate yourself, Lucinda. You are beautiful—in your own way.'

He said it quietly, with a certain amount of mockery, but Lucy suddenly felt foolishly happy. She tried to glance at herself surreptitiously in the shop windows as they passed but she didn't really need to. If Guy said she had a sort of beauty then she must have.

She wanted to cling to his hand but he didn't offer it. Instead he took her arm firmly. He knew where he was going and he had already said that he knew what he wanted, but then he always did. She wondered what she would look like after this little expedition.

It was no 'little' expedition. Guy took her to a very expensive salon and immediately models were drifting across Lucy's vision, showing fabulous clothes that she had never even imagined existed. Guy nodded or shook his head as a rather anxious-looking lady watched over this display. Alone, she would have intimidated Lucy, or anyone else for that matter, but Guy Chabrol had a monopoly on intimidation and his frequent dismissal of gowns, dresses and suits brought an atmosphere of anxiety to the whole place.

He nodded plenty of times though and Lucy dared not say anything at all. She wondered which of the selected ones he wanted her to have; they seemed to be piling up sky-high.

'I think that's enough to be going on with,' he finally announced, to the obvious relief of everyone. 'Now it is your turn to be a model, *ma chère.*'

She didn't remonstrate with him this time about calling her that and his smirk of amusement at her nervous glance passed right over her head.

'You—you want me to walk about and...?'

'*Mais naturellement!* I know how the garments look on these models but I am not about to buy them anything at all. I wish to know how they look on you.'

The manageress seemed to be praying silently that Lucy would behave herself and she was too overwhelmed to do anything else. She went to change and Guy settled back on the gilt chair to enjoy himself. This was his light entertainment, then? If her legs hadn't been trembling so much Lucy would have been very annoyed. As it was, she was simply embarrassed.

It soon passed, though. After the first appearance when she stood stiffly in front of Guy, turning like a wooden doll as he twirled his hand, her annoyance rose to the surface and helped enormously. She began to drift about as the models had done and Guy's narrowed, amused eyes told her that he noticed this small display of defiance.

She soon tired of it. Why couldn't he choose? Why hadn't he pointed and said, 'We'll take that one?'

'Splendid!' he announced as her defiance began to turn to exhaustion and the last garment was reached. '*Mademoiselle* will have everything she has tried. They are all suitable. Please deliver them this evening.'

'Yes, *Monsieur le Comte*. At once!'

'*All* of them?' Lucy whispered in horror, too taken up with the enormity of the purchases to keep quiet. 'I'll never wear even half of them!'

'Of course you will. You need even more. There are dinners to attend and we will also be entertaining. As my future wife you will be constantly with me. There is also the matter of a honeymoon. In any case, they will not fit you for long—when the baby is started.'

'Please don't talk about that!' Lucy begged urgently, her face flushed with embarrassment.

'I intend to do more than talk about it.'

'*Please!*'

'All in good time,' he murmured sardonically, nodding pleasantly to the greatly relieved manageress as she bowed them out of the salon. He glanced down at Lucy as they stepped into the street and he must have had his fill of light entertainment. He draped his arm across her shoulders and pulled her close.

'That is enough,' he said quietly. 'The battle is over, Lucinda. Today you have been transformed into my fiancée and tonight you will wear my ring. It is too late for hysterics.'

'I'm never hysterical,' Lucy muttered, very glad that he was holding her upright because she felt like sinking to the floor and staying there.

'No, you are not. You are a mixture of temper and shyness. You are given to strange actions and astonishing statements but you are never hysterical. Deep inside you have courage. It will not be needed. I will take care of you until this is all over. Until then we are in this together.'

If he wanted to depress her he was certainly going about it efficiently, Lucy thought. She began to think about what it would be like when she never saw him again but her mind shied away from it. She didn't want to think about that at all. There were lots of things she didn't want to think about but not seeing Guy again was the biggest dread in spite of this bargain.

She sighed and he glanced down at her, moving his protective arm and taking her hand.

'You are, however, given to bursts of drama,' he assured her in amusement. '*Viens, ma chère*, face the worst when it presents itself.'

'It did, the moment I first saw you,' Lucy said untruthfully.

He simply laughed and walked on but she was very glad that he held her hand warmly. It made her tingle inside and she had to really be firm with herself to stop clinging to him. He was clearly practising being engaged. She wished she were as good at acting.

He didn't bother to keep it up for long. After dinner he escorted her to his study, a huge room with a gold and white ceiling, and she was instantly nervous.

'I wish to place the ring on your finger,' he said impatiently when she stayed as far away from him as possible. 'Am I expected to chase you first? It would simplify matters if you could bring yourself to step closer.'

He watched her rather imperiously as she reluctantly approached and then he took her hand and slid a large diamond ring on to her finger.

'*Voilà!* You are now engaged. The first step towards your changed life is taken.'

As far as Lucy was concerned her life had changed long before this but he was right in one thing, it was a very definite step. It frightened her. There seemed to be little chance of escape now. It was so very final.

'I—I think you're going to regret this, *monsieur*,' she began quietly, avoiding his gaze.

It did nothing to lighten his mood, a mood that had been on him all evening.

'I am not going to regret it at all!' he rasped. 'I planned this and I know exactly what I am doing. The regret is all coming from you. No doubt you will remember to regret that your aunt is a thief?' He reached out and grasped her chin cruelly, jerking her face up, forcing her to meet eyes that blazed with annoyance. 'And *do not* call me *monsieur*! My name is Guy and you will say the name instead of this endless formality. I have told you that it will make Véronique suspicious.'

'I don't care! I can't go through with this!' Lucy snatched her chin away from the hard fingers and began to back off but his hands shot out and caught her.

'*Mon Dieu*, but you will go through with it!' he said explosively. 'I will make you!'

It was all the more alarming because he kept his voice low, his temper rumbling like a volcano. He seemed to be on the edge of a towering rage and Lucy stared into his dark eyes, her face white and shocked.

'You—you can't. Not—not really. If I stand up to you, you'll never——'

'Will I not?' he growled, pulling her forward. 'You imagine I'm about to call it all off and set you free? You were offered prison as an alternative and it is still there.' He let her go and turned away impatiently, every line of his body furious. 'You had better go before I lose all patience,' he snapped. 'No doubt Véronique would be willing to come up with a helpful story if I decided to get rid of you and let you face your fate. She is quite decided that you are unsuitable. To see the back of you would be something of a relief, I suspect.'

Lucy took his advice and made for the door speedily but he stopped her before she got there.

'There will be an engagement dinner at the end of this week,' he informed her aggressively, turning his dark face towards her. 'It will be your first dinner as my fiancée. Remember to wear your shoes, try not to fall over and you will manage quite well, I expect.'

'Now that I've been transformed!' Lucy managed tartly, her flushed face held proudly.

His eyes raked over her.

'You have not been transformed, *ma chère*,' he taunted. 'You have merely been polished a little. The mouse and the shrew are still there below the surface. See to it that the shrew does not raise its head at the engagement dinner. There will be important guests and I would not wish to see them shocked as I give you a good shaking.'

She could only glare at him and storm out but she didn't think he was too intimidated by her temper; his own was right at the top, boiling. It was difficult to understand him. Looking back he seemed to be constantly moving between a sort of kindness and a wild rage. This afternoon he had been mocking, it was true, but all in all he had been gentle, he had even held her hand.

Since then, however, he had been smouldering with anger. All the time at dinner he had watched her closely, his dark eyes cold, his face stiff with some sort of annoyance, and now he was in a real rage although nothing had changed. After all, he had already known he was going to give her the ring. She wondered where he had got it from. Had he shopped for that while she was with Véronique?

Lucy shook herself out of these useless speculations and went to her room. She had more to worry about than the ring. How was she going to manage a glittering dinner in this château? How could she possibly pass as the future wife of a count?

* * *

As it turned out, she managed very well. Her natural shyness gave her a very quiet dignity that was no doubt mistaken by some for aloofness. Whatever they thought, it seemed to please Guy. After a few taut moments when he was clearly on edge he relaxed and even looked as if he was enjoying himself. He rarely left her side and, when he did, Véronique was there at once, also pleased, so pleased that she smiled a great deal. The servants beamed on her, the lights glittered and in one of the dresses that Guy had chosen, a white silk shift, the skirt tasselled with gold, she felt fairly secure.

She was with Véronique when late guests arrived, a young woman and an obviously older man. They spoke to Guy and then came straight across and Lucy noted that Guy did not this time hurry to join her.

'So at last he's getting married?' The woman smiled in a conspiratorial way at Véronique and then turned assessing eyes on Lucy. 'I had begun to think it would never happen. You must have the magic touch, *mademoiselle*. Guy is a confirmed bachelor.'

'Not any more,' Lucy said quietly. She could feel an atmosphere here. Véronique had stiffened considerably and across the room she could feel Guy's eyes burning into her.

'I am amazed that nobody knows about you, *mademoiselle*. I do not even know your name with any certainty. I am Michelle Colliot.'

'Perhaps you didn't read the invitation too clearly,' Lucy suggested quietly. There had been a very subtle dismissal in the woman's voice, as if Lucy were of no consequence except for her involvement in the unusual event of Guy getting married. 'My name is Lucinda Balfour. I don't suppose people have had time to hear about me yet. I haven't known Guy for very long.'

'A whirlwind courtship?' Michelle Colliot looked slightly sceptical.

'Love at first sight,' Lucy assured her seriously, feeling that she must defend herself speedily. It went down very heavily and Michelle did not linger.

Véronique took Lucy's arm and turned her away just as Guy came up.

'Time for me to escort you to dinner, Lucinda.' He smiled down at her, but it looked to Lucy as if it was a bit of an effort. She was captured, though, and Guy's hand slid up her arm, pulling her close.

'What did Michelle want to talk about?' he asked a little sharply.

'Our whirlwind romance.'

He drew back and looked at her, his black brows drawn together, anger glittering in his eyes. 'I asked you a civil question. Answer properly!'

'It may have been a civil question but it wasn't asked very civilly and, in any case, I'm telling the truth. She was astonished that I'd captured you.' Lucy looked up at him pertly. 'I had to confess that it was love at first sight. That satisfied her.'

'If you are beginning to——' His anger was barely contained but the room was filled with people, many of them looking across at the 'happy' couple, and Lucy looked straight at Guy with defiance right at the surface.

'If I am beginning to misbehave you'll shake me?' she enquired crisply. 'Go ahead. It will bring some life into the party. I'm bored out of my mind.'

For a second he stared into her wide blue eyes and then he relaxed, his lips quirking.

'Little wretch,' he murmured softly. '*Mon Dieu!* You are not as easy to manage as I imagined at first. I will have to train you.'

'Never in a month of Sundays!' Lucy retorted, gasping as his arm came around her waist, his hand curving round her hip. It sent shock waves right through her but when she looked up he was no longer amused. His eyes were on Michelle Colliot, who was looking at him with dark, possessive eyes. She looked at him all the way through dinner, too, and evidently Véronique noticed. She was back by Lucy's side after dinner the moment that Guy left her.

'I hope that Michelle does not attempt to upset you, Lucinda,' she said in a low voice. 'She is very spoiled and at one time imagined that she would be the next Comtesse de Chauvrais.'

'What happened?' Lucy asked quietly, her eyes searching for Guy.

'She married Albert Colliot. He is wealthy and easy to handle, much older than Michelle. Guy has the wealth but has never been easy to handle—not that he wished to marry her,' she added hastily, her face flushing.

Lucy doubted that. Guy was standing across the room, talking to a group of people, but his eyes were intently on Michelle who seemed to be well aware of the fact.

Later, as she danced with Guy, Lucy felt the woman's eyes on her and she turned, not missing the malevolence.

'Somebody doesn't like me,' she observed brightly.

'Who could possibly dislike you?' Guy growled impatiently. 'You behave very well except with me.'

'Nobody has trapped me, except you,' Lucy reminded him. 'I was speaking of Madame Colliot, as a matter of fact. She still seems unconvinced that this is real. Maybe it's because she wanted to marry you herself.'

Guy snapped at her, his hands tightening painfully, 'As you can see, she is already married. In any case, I have told you, it is not my intention to marry in any real capacity. Women are treacherous and good for one thing only. This marriage is merely to get an heir. Surely you don't need to be reminded of that?' he added sardonically, waiting cruelly for her usual blushes to surface.

They didn't; she was too busy working out that to marry Michelle would now be impossible as she was already married. Véronique imagined that Guy had never asked her, or at least she had hastily said that. Lucy thought otherwise. He had spoken about faithless women. The mystery was solved. He loved Michelle and she had turned him down. No wonder he didn't want a permanent wife if he still loved another woman.

'What are you thinking?' Guy tilted her face that had suddenly lost its life.

'My thoughts are private. You didn't buy those,' Lucy said bitterly, feeling cold and inexplicably lost.

'I have not yet bought anything, except a few clothes,' he reminded her quietly, his dark eyes intently on her face. 'I am not buying you either. It is a job, just like any other job, one that will benefit us both.'

'No doubt.' She turned away from his eyes, lowering her head, and his hand came around her nape as he held her more closely. It was warm, comforting, but it was probably for the benefit of onlookers, especially Michelle.

'Somebody has upset you, Lucinda?' he asked softly, his face against her hair.

'Nobody at all. I'm simply in the middle of a nightmare and, from time to time, I realise it.'

Her words and her tight voice had the desired effect. He withdrew his hand and held her less warmly, not warmly at all in fact. For the rest of the evening he was cold as ice, black anger just below the surface, and Lucy was glad when it was all over and they stood together seeing the guests out.

'You are a lucky man, *Monsieur le Comte*,' Albert Colliot said as they left. 'An unusual English bride with skin like velvet and a face like that of a beautiful fawn. You make a handsome couple.'

'She is not a bride yet, *chéri*,' Michelle said, with a sidelong glance at Guy.

'She will be,' Guy assured her in a caustic voice. 'She is an enchantress. Clearly your husband sees it himself. How could I let her escape me?' He had the last word, of course, but then he usually did.

'You should have married her,' Lucy muttered angrily as they walked back across the huge hall, the last of the guests gone.

'Who?' He looked down at her coldly.

'Michelle. Isn't it obvious?'

'Have I ever told you that you are ridiculous?' he grated, coming to a halt and grabbing her arm tightly.

'Not that I recall.' She looked up at him with miserable defiance, but he didn't see the misery.

'Then it was an oversight. I will correct that now. You are ridiculous!'

'Not really,' Lucy pointed out. 'Just hopeful. Even at the last minute I'm praying that someone will take my place.'

'Like a married woman, for example?' he asked savagely.

'Marriages can end. Ours will. It's something to look forward to.'

His grip tightened and she wondered for a moment if she had gone too far. Misery that had been growing steadily had sharpened her tongue and she had forgotten for a moment that he was capable of wild rage. He controlled it with difficulty.

'Go to bed, Mademoiselle Balfour, before I forget that I am a civilised man and beat you soundly!' he snapped. His eyes suddenly narrowed on her pale face. 'But then, perhaps you would not care as you are bored out of your mind.'

Lucy snatched her arm away and walked off up the wide stairs, aware that his eyes were burning into her straight back. She didn't care. He was cruel, merciless. Hadn't she known that right from the first? She looked at herself in the long mirror in her luxurious room. Her face was almost as white as the dress, her eyes too big in her face. An enchantress? She didn't think so, and neither did he. Michelle was not convinced either. She wondered if Guy still saw her secretly? No. He wouldn't, it would be beneath his dignity. He remembered, though, that was very obvious. She wondered why it made her feel so unhappy. She had enough to feel unhappy about without anything else added to it.

Guy came to the door when she was ready for bed and she answered because she thought it was Véronique. He stood looking at her as she opened the door and she felt a twinge of alarm although the anger had left his face.

'What do you want?' She stood in her dressing-gown and regarded him solemnly.

'I have come to apologise. You are not ridiculous. I have told you that I find you amusing and often quite charming.'

'Thank you,' Lucy said stiffly. 'Goodnight.'

His hand came to the door as she made to close it quickly and he smiled at her look of alarm.

'I am not about to enter and put you out of your misery, Lucinda,' he said with some amusement.

'I'm glad to hear it,' she got out breathlessly. 'I'd scream the place down.'

'Will you do that on our honeymoon?' He was inside the room before she could make a move to stop him. 'You have not screamed thus far when I have kissed you. I want to kiss you goodnight to show that I am not angry and to thank you for the great effort you made this evening.'

'Praise is sufficient,' Lucy said breathlessly, backing off.

He reached out and collected her to him, closing the door and leaning back against it, pulling her close.

'Perhaps it is not sufficient for me,' he murmured. 'Come here, Lucinda. It is time you had some practice in being engaged.'

'No!' She struggled belatedly but it was altogether too late. He pulled her closer, his lips searching for hers, and as he kissed her she stopped struggling. It seemed impossible to struggle any more. His fingers raked through her hair, clasping her head to hold her face to his, his lips searching hers more deeply than they had ever done before and this time she felt the heat sear through her and recognised it. It was desire; her misery before, jealousy.

She softened and he brought her tightly against him, shocking her as she felt the surge of his body against hers.

'You are surprised that I want you?' he murmured against her ear, his hand cupping her head. 'Do you imagine I could make this kind of bargain with a woman I did not desire at all? I have said you are an enchantress. You are. You are unusual, elusive, a challenge.'

For seconds she was dreamy, dazed with feelings she had only vaguely felt before and he took advantage of her enchantment, his lips moving over her face and neck before fusing with hers again as he wrapped her tightly to him, forcing her to accept an almost angry desire.

It was sheer magic until she allowed reason to creep in. Of course he needed to make her believe he wanted her. It was probably easy for a man. Michelle's face swam into her mind, that and the fact that she was merely a very peculiar employee.

She pulled away, standing free, her chest heaving with a pain that seemed to be spreading all the way through her.

'Please go away!' she managed shakily, making herself look up to meet angry, narrowed eyes.

'And if I do not?' He stared into her eyes menacingly and she flushed, her skin like a wild rose.

'I'll scream for Véronique.'

'You imagine I would let you?'

His eyes roamed over her face, his gaze narrowed and burning. He looked so fierce, so cruel, that she felt a wave of fear and he saw it, his own face tightening further.

'I assured you that there would be no need to fear me,' he grated.

'You're convincing me that there is,' Lucy managed. 'I'm not a fool. I know why you're here. Seeing Michelle Colliot upset you, didn't it? Well, you're not taking it out on me!'

She was momentarily off guard, too busy fighting jealousy to care, and he drew her roughly to him, kissing her harshly this time, his mouth open and demanding, not coaxing any more. He let her go when she felt too weak to stand and then he glared at her.

'I take back my apology,' he snapped. 'You *are* ridiculous after all!'

He was gone before she could recover and she almost fell on the door, locking it and leaning against it, halfway between tears and yearning. She would not be able to lock the door on their honeymoon and he would be ruthless. Her hands balled into fists, coming to her hot face, and she began to pace the room, quite sure that she would be doing that for the rest of the night.

CHAPTER SEVEN

DURING the following days, Lucy did a lot of soul-searching. She was caught up in Guy's life and unable to break free. At the beginning she had sometimes doubted whether he would carry out his threat if she either left or attempted to back out of the bargain. Now she was in little doubt. He was darkly silent, verging on anger every time he looked at her. His looks too were frequent, so frequent and so brooding that she was sure he regretted this as much as she did, but his plans were inflexible and he had made his announcement to more than the family.

The whole of the household seemed to be vigorously involved in preparing for the wedding and Véronique was in a state of tight nerves, her face too strained to do much smiling. Guy appeared to do nothing—except watch Lucy narrowly whenever they were in the same room. He rarely spoke to her unless there were others present and seemed to go out of his way to avoid any sort of contact.

Escape was impossible unless she walked out of the château and begged a lift, because although he had spent what appeared to be a fortune on clothes for her, he had made quite sure she had no cash at all, and so had Aunt Wanda for that matter. As cash had always been a scarce commodity in her family, Lucy had not given it any consideration. She did now, but it was too late. She was not about to risk her life begging lifts from strangers, however.

She tried telling herself that this was merely an arranged marriage, but Guy's cool logic didn't help much. She could never have a child and then abandon it. She would end up begging to stay and she knew Guy's ruthless thoughts on that score. He didn't trust women, especially those who were clinging.

'You are to be taken to choose a wedding gown.' Guy's announcement stopped Lucy in her tracks as she walked in the garden. He had come out to join her to make this statement and she looked up at him as calmly as possible. His presence seemed to dominate her, an almost deliberate air of menace about him.

'I thought I had plenty of nice dresses.'

She let mutiny well up to cover panic. There was a finality about it. The wedding gown, then the wedding, then... Her face was pale and his eyes narrowed in disapproval.

'You need a wedding gown, not a dress. It will be a society wedding and you will be under considerable scrutiny.' He spoke curtly, staring at her coldly. 'In any case,' he added impatiently, 'the clothes you chose when you were with me are not "dresses", they are also gowns.'

'I didn't choose them,' Lucy reminded him. 'You chose them. As to dresses or gowns, I don't know any better, do I? They're all frocks to me.'

'It is how they look on you,' he sneered. 'However, we have done our best. Perhaps other people will be taken in long enough for us to get this thing over with.'

He took one satisfied look at her distressed face and then left, and those few insulting words made her mind up for her. She was in her room within minutes, her clothes thrown on to the bed, her canvas grip that she had stubbornly refused to be parted from being stuffed with her own things. She would get away if she had to work as a kitchen maid in Paris until she had her fare. She was angry that she hadn't done it before. Guy was mesmerising her. Well, he wouldn't get the chance now! If somebody kidnapped her on the way, well, so much for that! Wasn't she kidnapped now?

She didn't take one single item that Guy had bought and she left the wardrobe doors wide open to prove it. He wasn't going to be able to say she helped her aunt to steal and then also stole clothes. As to the police, if he called them, she would hide out, sneak about like Guy did. She was so angry and insulted that it all seemed possible.

Nobody knew her except the few people she had met at the dinner party and the servants here, and with this thought clearly in her head she made her way downstairs stealthily, her eyes wide and alert on the closed doors that led off the great magnificent hall.

There was nobody about. Guy would be in his study, brooding and seething, no doubt, and Véronique had probably taken herself off to bed with a headache after all the strain. The fresh air was a tonic and she skirted the lake at the back, her eyes anxiously on the study window, her breath almost held until she was into the woods at the side of the lake.

She had explored this area plenty of times since she had been here and she made for the path that led to the long winding drive. Today the florist's van had come to the château, the assistant carrying in great flower arrangements for Madame Gatien to put into place. She had seen him from her window but he had never seen her. She glanced at her watch. Soon his van would come back towards the village. She would beg a lift.

The van almost took her by surprise as she trudged along deep in gloom. He was going fast but she stepped out and waved frantically and to her relief he stopped, his eyes peering at her speculatively. It gave her pause for thought, but if she could deal with Guy she could deal with anybody.

'Can you give me a lift, *monsieur*?' She made no attempt to stammer out her non-existent French and he grinned at her cheekily.

'*Oui, mademoiselle*. Where do you want me to lift you to?'

The fact that he spoke English was such a relief that she almost ignored his innuendo and the look in his eyes. She became prim once she was inside the van.

'I would like a ride to Paris, but if you're not going that far, then anywhere on the way,' she said firmly.

'You work at the château, *mademoiselle*?' He let in the clutch and she breathed more easily. She was on her way.

'Not any more. I—er—I've been there for a while but the count is back now and my services aren't needed. I'm going home.'

'I'm surprised he did not give you transport, *mademoiselle*. He is a very generous man and well liked. Still, they say he is getting married to a very beautiful English girl. Perhaps he is too involved with her to remember his obligations?'

'Yes,' Lucy muttered. It was the first time she had been called a very beautiful English girl. It was easy to understand as nobody had seen her.

'You are English too. What a coincidence.'

'Yes. I—er—I've been a maid to the countess but I don't speak French and I think she got tired of speaking English. She's getting a French maid.'

He nodded and lapsed into silence and she was glad of it. She was glad too that his original speculative looks had subsided. She could well do without an amorous Frenchman on this lonely road.

In the village he stopped, smiling reassuringly at her small gasp of dismay.

'It is all right, *mademoiselle*. I am going to Paris and I will take you there. I have just realised that there was

to be another delivery and I have no address. I must
contact my office. I will be no more than a moment.'

Lucy subsided thankfully. A lift into Paris. At least
she was able to get that far. As Guy had been unwilling
to be anywhere near her recently he wouldn't find out
about her disappearance before dinner and by then she
could be on her way again, perhaps with Paris behind
her.

Maybe he would just be glad to see the back of her?
She looked down at her hands folded in her lap and saw
how tight they were, how tense. It was no relief to feel
that Guy would be glad to see her go. The life seemed
to have gone out of her with every mile that distanced
her from him and she remembered that, even at this
château, the day had been spent in waiting for a glimpse
of him even though he was usually frowning.

It was a pretty hopeless muddle and she would just
have to put it out of her mind as she had put so many
things out of her mind in her life. She knew perfectly
well how she felt about Guy but there was no future in
it at all.

She looked up and saw the driver coming towards her.
He was just sauntering along. She wished he would get
a move on. She wanted to be miles from here before Guy
realised she had left. He wasn't just sauntering along;
he was dawdling, stopping to speak to people who looked
as if they had better things to do, and Lucy watched him
impatiently, quite irritated by the time he got himself to
the van and started the engine.

'Did you have another delivery?'

'No, it was cancelled.'

Lucy was pleased to hear it; any more hanging about
and she was going to be stuck in Paris at night-time,
with little chance of a further lift. He set off and went
so slowly that she could have shaken him but she
resolutely kept quiet, beggars not being choosers, and

she even managed to stay calm when he began to sing under his breath, a discordant sound that set her teeth on edge.

They were a few miles along the road to Paris when a large black Mercedes shot past and drew in in front of them with all lights flashing and Lucy sank low in her seat as Guy got out and slammed the door, stalking threateningly back towards the van. The driver didn't wait for him to arrive. He got out, his deceitful face covered with smiles.

'I have her safely, *Monsieur le Comte*,' he announced smugly. 'I hope I did the right thing?'

'You did.' Guy dived into his back pocket and handed over what looked like a large roll of notes, waving aside the driver's protests. 'Take it. I am grateful. She means everything to me and a silly quarrel has brought this about. I am glad she chose to beg a lift with you. Not all people are so trustworthy.'

Lucy got out, her eyes stormily on the van driver.

'You——!' She opened her mouth to tell him exactly what she thought but Guy intervened quickly.

'Come home, *chérie*,' he said, before she could get out more than the one word. 'I was terrified when I found you gone. No more quarrels. If I lost you I would not want to live.'

His arms came round her and she could feel threat there, his eyes too were menacing. If she said one word to let the driver know the true state of affairs no doubt Guy would strangle her. She kept quiet and allowed herself to be led away, her eyes carefully avoiding the driver.

Guy lost no time in turning the car and heading back for the château, and the last glimpse she had of her betrayer was the sight of him counting his money with a look closely akin to astonishment on his face.

Guy said nothing. His silence was as alarming as his expression and Lucy sat tensely on the very edge of the seat. At the château, he got out and came to help her, his actions outwardly chivalrous but the tight hand on her arm telling her that he would not take any more nonsense.

'My grip!' She stopped as he led her forward but his hand did not slacken.

'It will stay there. This evening I will get it for you. If there is anything in it that you desperately need then you will have to manage. I am not about to inform the whole staff that you were fleeing. It is more than enough that the delivery man knows. Let us hope that the ransom I paid for you will keep him quiet.'

'It wasn't a ransom, it was a bribe!' Lucy informed him. In fact she was in a state of total dismay. At the sight of him as he had furiously approached the van, her heart had leapt, not with fright but with excitement and even now, with his hand hard on her arm, she was flooded with warmth and a sinking feeling of gladness.

He led her straight to her room, coming in with her and locking the door and her eyes went from the door to his tight face.

'Why have you done that? What are you——?'

'I am not about to beat you, *mademoiselle*,' he assured her caustically, advancing on her steadily, his dark eyes narrowed on her frantic face. 'I am about to do what I should have done a long time ago.'

'What—what's that? What do you mean?'

Lucy retreated as he advanced but he came on steadily until her retreat ended, the wall by the window hard against her back.

'I am about to put you out of your misery, *ma chère*.'

She just stared at him and his dark, probing gaze made her nerves tighten, her flesh beginning to tingle even before he touched her. She felt the colour drain from her face and his lips curved cruelly, his eyes burningly intent.

'What did you expect?' he enquired in a low voice. 'You almost managed to escape, to abandon the bargain and leave me without a wife. It is fortunate that the driver recognised you.'

'He—he didn't!' Lucy stammered, thankful he had stopped and was just standing looking at her. 'I—I told him I was a maid.'

'Then why did he telephone me and say that he had my future wife in his van?'

'I—I don't know. Maybe it was because I'm English. He didn't know me though. He said that you were going to marry a beautiful English girl, so he thought that——'

'You do not know that you are beautiful, Lucinda?' he asked mockingly and her face flooded with colour, her eyes downcast.

'I know I'm not. Don't be cruel, Guy. I can't take any more.'

'I have already told you that in your own way you are beautiful,' he reminded her softly, his eyes raking over her face. 'Unusual and challenging, your pert little face defiant, your blue eyes wide and bewildered. Your beauty is a temptation, *mademoiselle*.'

'Why do you keep calling me that?' she breathed fretfully, sanity beginning to leave her. There was an electric current of feeling flashing between them and she knew it wasn't all coming from her. Did he really want her, after all?

'What do you want me to call you? You want me to say, Lucy?'

'Yes. No! I—I don't know...'

'We will find out.'

He reached for her slowly and she had plenty of time to resist but she didn't. It was as if fate had decreed that she should meet Guy and be unable to escape. She was numb with the inevitability of it and her eyes closed as his hand slid beneath her hair to close warmly around her nape.

Feelings flooded through her, her lower limbs beginning to melt towards him as a soft, velvet warmth raced from the very core of her being.

'I can't help it.'

She thought the words were in her mind only but Guy's dark head lifted as his lips had begun to close over hers and his eyes burned into her own. She just gazed back and saw a flicker of something that was not scorn. It looked like a flare of excitement. His face darkened and he drew her completely into his arms.

'Why try to?' he murmured. 'Your fate was decided the moment I saw you.'

She argued in her head. No, not the moment you saw me. You looked at me as if you despised me. It was only when the idea came to you, when you knew I wasn't a thief that you decided... It was all so much madness. A cruel trap.

'No!' She struggled, but his reaction was swift; he swept her up into his arms, kissing her harshly.

'Yes!' His lips closed over hers again, very different from the other times he had kissed her. His mouth was hungry, parting her lips, probing, cruel, moving over hers expertly. She felt the softness of the bed beneath her as he lowered her to it and came down with her, his body almost covering hers.

Her small cries were lost against his hard lips and he kissed her until her struggling hands subsided against his chest and then crept up to cling around his neck helplessly. She wanted to be here with Guy. No amount of denial would alter the fact.

Salty tears escaped from beneath her lashes and mixed with his kisses and he relaxed his cruel grip, his tongue catching the tears like some pagan ritual.

'Perhaps I cannot help it either,' he breathed against her mouth. 'Perhaps I do not wish to find out if I can.'

She felt his body harden against her own and reality left her almost completely. She softened to him, exciting him further, and his hands twisted in her hair as he raised her face.

'Now, *ma chère,*' he said thickly. 'Now we will dispose of your fears. Now, Lucy.'

Somehow the sound of her name on his lips, especially in that dark, hoarse voice, sent a shudder racing through her. Desire tore through her, recognisable now, sweet and thrilling, and she moaned aloud, trying to release herself from this torture, but he seemed to have expected it and there was no release.

'No, Lucy. It is time. I want you.'

His mouth was urgent, something wild winging between them, and she was almost panic-stricken at the pounding of her own heart, at the heat that passed through them like a fire generated from deep inside each of them.

'Guy!' She gasped his name against his lips and he brought her more tightly to him, his movement almost savage, his hands caressing her body with restless, urgent movements, his fingers searching her back beneath her sweater. His hands moved upwards, the sweater moving with them and anxiety raced back into her mind. She had never worn a bra. To her it was as restrictive as shoes had been and now he would know. She murmured, her body freezing, but he was relentless and the sweater slid over her head with hardly any pause in the kiss.

His hands closed over her breasts, roughly caressing, and excitement surged through her veins like wine as a

startled cry left her lips. He lowered his head, his white
teeth closing experimentally over the tight pink nipple,
nipping her erotically before his mouth soothed the sharp
pain.

'Why did you run away?' He raised his head and
looked down at her flushed face. 'You imagined it would
be like this on our wedding night, savage, frightening?'

She shook her head. It wasn't frightening. The only
thing frightening her was her own feelings. She couldn't
look away from the dark eyes that held hers and his hand
closed over her breast, his fingers caressing as he watched
her face.

'Feelings have only just begun. What will you do when
they get stronger?'

She couldn't answer and she realised that she was
shaking, grateful when his eyes stopped probing her mind
as his lips brushed hers.

'You want me,' he murmured darkly. 'You ran from
me and yet you want me badly. I have done what no
man has ever done. I have awakened you. You want me
to make love to you and never stop. You think you are
not beautiful?' He raised his head and looked at the high,
rosy peaks his hands caressed. 'Your skin is like pearl,
pearl topped by rosebuds. You taste sweet, fresh,
honeyed.' To prove it his lips covered her breast, tasting
and arousing, and she melted limply towards him,
helpless, drowning in emotion, a terrible hunger growing
inside her as he satisfied his desire to taste her.

'Oh! Please! No!'

As his hands found the zip of her skirt and slid it
downwards she flinched anew, confused by the shattering of every thought she had ever had about this, but
he simply ignored her gasps of fear, his hands freeing
her skirt and letting it slide to the floor. He lifted her
and his tongue traced streaks of fire across her stomach,

a low tormented growl of sound deep in his throat as his teeth bit gently into her hip.

He raised his head, his eyes probing hers, probing her mind as he saw the languid fascination she felt under his caresses.

'I want to take you now, to settle your foolish fears,' he murmured thickly, his eyes hotly roaming over her breasts. 'But this marriage will be legal, my heir legitimate. It will not be a dry as dust marriage, though. That was a mistaken idea. I will enjoy our wedding night, and so will you. You feel part of what a woman is supposed to feel and we have not even begun.'

He stood, looking down at her for a moment as she lay aching and bewildered, and then he strode to the door, unlocking it and turning to look back at her as she raised herself on her elbows and stared at him like someone hypnotised.

'Do not attempt to run away from me again,' he threatened darkly, his glance flaring over her. One brown finger jabbed the air, pointing at her and emphasising his rasped order. 'And do not again tell me that you are not beautiful. It is for me to decide and I have decided. When you come down to dinner I expect to see a woman, not a frightened mouse. If you are a shrew, I will return to this room with you after dinner and set your mind right again.'

He left and she subsided on to the soft sheets, her eyes on the ceiling, waves of aching rapture racing through her. She was alive, awake, restless with longing. Her lips still felt his tasting her, her body felt the warmth, the strength of his arms. She rolled from the bed to her feet, her hand clenched to her mouth. It was an arrangement, a bargain, nothing more. It would never be anything more but her ability to leave him had all drained away.

She went down to dinner feeling searingly alive, but with her eyes unknowingly showing her bruised feelings.

Guy turned impatiently away when she refused a drink and avoided his gaze and her eyes followed him almost mournfully.

Even if this had been real, even if he had wanted to marry her with no ulterior motive, how would she have ever been able to cope with him, with his passions and his strange burning tempers? Common sense, of which she had plenty, would never make up for her lack of knowledge of a man like Guy. He would be bored with her rapidly.

As it was, this was a bargain for a little time and her heart felt heavy when she thought of the time to leave. A baby seemed an unlikely dream. It would never happen.

'You need not fear a repetition of this afternoon,' Guy rasped as she almost cringed away from him when they moved from the dining table to take coffee. Véronique was watching them with an undue fascination and Lucy knew that her new feelings were swimming to the surface every few minutes, showing on her face.

He walked abruptly out of the dining-room ahead of them and Véronique sat next to Lucy as coffee was served.

'I suppose Guy has told you about the wedding arrangements?' she asked quietly.

'I have not!' Guy answered before she could speak. 'Time enough to terrify her when it is necessary.'

'She will have to face it, Guy,' Véronique said impatiently. 'After all, she's going to be there.' It was a feeble joke, made because Véronique was well aware of the atmosphere between them. It did not amuse Guy.

'I sometimes wonder about that,' he muttered, pouring himself another drink and slumping into a chair with ill-concealed irritation. 'She would like to fall asleep and wake when it is all over!'

'Guy!' Véronique looked scandalised and her eyes went nervously to Lucy, who was fighting back tears. Guy followed her glance.

'Do not panic, Véronique. She will face it. She will not walk out, will you, *ma chère*?'

There was an exquisite threat in his voice and Lucy looked at him with flushed cheeks, her head thrown up proudly, her eyes glistening with tears.

'I'm destined to be a countess,' she stated flatly and his mouth twisted ironically as he looked at her, Véronique ignored.

'You are. I'm sure you can think of other things much more alarming.' There was a fraught silence and then Véronique interrupted it quite breathlessly.

'Yes. Well, I'd better enlighten you as Guy has not done so.' There was a trace of anxiety in her voice and Lucy glanced at Guy. His dark face was aloof, stern, unbending, and she felt a wave of fright. How had he managed to get her to melt in his arms? He was the most tightly controlled, the most strict man she would ever meet. He looked up and caught her eyes on him and his expression deepened from coldness to anger as he stood.

'I will leave you two ladies to discuss wedding details,' he snapped as he walked out without waiting for any reply.

Lucy's face was miserable. She was simply a pawn in this, being moved this way and that at Guy's whim. Véronique must have had the same thought because she looked suddenly embarrassed and began to talk almost gushingly. Lucy would rather not have known. She didn't want a history of the weddings of past Comtes de Chauvrais. She didn't want to know about the small but exquisite cathedral or the three hundred guests. By the time she escaped to bed she was almost shaking with fright and she almost wished that Guy had been waiting

for her in her room to entrance her out of it no matter
how savagely. He was not.

On the day she was too numb to feel anything at all.
Guy had not approached her again and it had been left
to Véronique to manage things. At the rehearsal, Guy
had helped, but it was only that she had set her mind
steadfastly to getting through the actual ceremony, to
remembering everything, that had enabled her to go
through with it.

When the day itself arrived she was almost immune
to anything. The hundreds of guests were simply a sea
of faces, people she didn't know, people she would never
see again. Her mind noted Michelle Colliot, the beautiful face cold and tight, but her feet took her to Guy
and he turned and held out his hand, his dark eyes
meeting hers for a second and then it was all out of her
control. The ceremony began and she was committed,
committed to Guy for as long as this bargain needed to
last, sacrificed for Guy's plans and her own inability to
break free of him.

The walk down the aisle to the joyous peal of bells
brought tears to the back of her eyes and as they stood
and received congratulations Guy's arm came tightly
around her.

'It is almost over,' he whispered against her hair, suddenly comforting. 'You have managed well. Do not let
me down now.'

'I'm not going to.' She closed her eyes for a second
and his arm tightened.

'I hear your tears, Lucinda, even though they are
silent. It is for a little time only, and then you will be
more free than you have ever been in your life.'

She didn't answer. He could not have said anything
to distress her more, because while she had stood before
the altar with him she had almost drifted into a dream

that this was real, never to end. Tears choked her but she held them inside. She would be rich and truly more free than she had ever been before. She would be more alone too. The crowds of guests didn't matter any more. There were other priorities. The end could not come soon enough for her because with every day that passed she was becoming more and more ensnared by Guy Chabrol.

Michelle came up to them as they stood with other guests and she slid her arm into Guy's.

'Married! I never thought I would see the day, *chéri*. I suppose it had to happen sooner or later.'

'I waited for the right woman,' he informed her a little tightly, extricating his arm. It merely amused Michelle.

'You must have changed. Innocence never really appealed to you.'

'There's not a great deal of it available. I am lucky.'

'So you are,' Michelle answered, looking up at him with sparkling eyes. 'Innocence at home and excitement further afield. I imagine your business trips will not be dull.'

'They will not. Lucinda will be there,' Guy said tauntingly, and Michelle turned and walked off.

Lucy was not at all in doubt about what Michelle meant. It was so obvious that they had been lovers; maybe they still were. Michelle was bitterly hurt by Guy's marriage. It was written across her face.

'I don't like this,' she said tremulously, her face pale.

'You imagine that I do?' He looked down at her mockingly. 'You do not know me, *ma chère*, and you will never know me. Do not trouble your head about it. It will not concern you for long. You can afford to ignore Michelle. She is not the Comtesse de Chauvrais.' He looked round impatiently. 'One more hour of this to endure, I think, and then we can leave them behind.'

'Leave them?' Panic flared in Lucy and she looked at him anxiously, a fact that seemed to give him cause for caustic amusement.

'They are most certainly not invited on our honeymoon,' he mocked. 'Honeymoons are for two people only, the bride and the groom. We will not need guests.'

A shiver flared over her skin.

'When...? Where...? How...?' she began breathlessly and Guy smiled for the first time that day.

'When? In one hour. Where? Sicily. How? By air. By tonight, we will be safely away from all this, and alone.' He looked at her tauntingly and she looked hastily away, her heart taking off at an alarming rate. Alone? Perhaps. Safely? She thought not!

Véronique came in to see her as she was changing to leave for Paris.

'You—you looked very nice, Lucinda,' she said hesitantly. 'It all went off very well. Guy must have been proud of you, being as you are—er—unaccustomed to this sort of thing.'

'Is anyone ever really accustomed to this sort of thing?' Lucy asked quietly. 'Are you? Did you like all the ceremony, the strain, the crowds of people?'

Véronique blinked rapidly, a small nervous habit she had that came out when she was a little dumbfounded.

'No. No, I suppose you're right. Nobody in their right mind would like to face this sort of thing regularly.' She suddenly laughed, the first time Lucy had ever seen genuine laughter in this woman. 'We managed it, though, didn't we? I wonder if Guy thought we wouldn't be able to cope?'

She gave Lucy an unexpected kiss on her cheek as she left.

'Have a lovely time,' she said quietly. 'Sicily is beautiful, especially Taormina, where Guy is taking you. I went there too, with his father.' She looked saddened, but before Lucy could say anything she was gone and Guy appeared at the door like a dark magician, ready to spirit her away.

Their eyes met and then his gaze roamed over her as she stood in her green silk suit, her eyes suddenly downcast.

'Like an angel awaiting her fate,' he murmured. He held out his hand. 'Come along, countess, let us leave with a flourish. There are still about two hundred guests waiting to see us off.'

And one of them Michelle Colliot, Lucy thought. She gave him her hand, she had no alternative, and as she walked down to confront the sea of faces, now upturned towards her, she just let them all blend, anaesthetising her mind. If he still loved Michelle it didn't matter, because this was all pretend, a marriage with a good reason, Guy's reason. He didn't belong to her. He would never belong to anyone, not now. If he loved Michelle it was too late anyway.

CHAPTER EIGHT

TAORMINA sat high above the sea, a long sweep of glorious coastline and Mount Etna unmistakable and forbidding to the west. The streets were lined with cafés, and little piazzas with shops caught the eye. The air was balmy—almost sensuous—and there were flowers everywhere. The luxurious hotel where they were to stay seemed to be full of them, and, for a brief time, Lucy was so entranced that she forgot to be nervous at all.

They had a suite of rooms with views of the great horseshoe curve of the bay, of towering rocks edged by white sand, and Lucy stood at the window gazing her fill as the luggage was brought up and Guy dealt with the porters.

'You find it beautiful?'

He was behind her and she instinctively stiffened, her enjoyment dulled at once, but she managed a calm-voiced reply.

'Very beautiful. I—I've never lived by the sea in England. It's very special to be able to just stand and look at it.'

'Not for too long if we are to eat. The flight was late and I'm told that dinner is almost finished. We had better go down now, I think. You can gaze at the sea later.'

It gave her an excuse to move away.

'I'll just freshen up.' She shot a rather nervous glance at him and he nodded curtly, his lips tightening at her obvious desire to put some distance between them. When she came from the bathroom he was pacing abou't, no† looking at anything, his hands deep in his pockets, and for a moment she felt he had forgotten she was there.

'I'm ready. Shall we go down?'

Lucy stood demurely waiting and his dark eyes swept over her with what looked very much like distaste.

'We may as well. I cannot think of any reason to postpone the meal.'

'Do—do I look all right?' Guy might be used to places like this but she wasn't, in fact the only time in her life she had been in any sort of hotel was when she had flown to Paris with her aunt.

'You wish me to tell you again that you are beautiful? I am not given to offering countless compliments. If you were not "all right" I would tell you.'

He turned abruptly away and opened the outer door of the suite, not speaking at all, and Lucy hurried forwards, depression rising inside her when she thought of the coming night. He wasn't even going to be civil during the meal. The night would be a nightmare she just would not be able to face.

She had enough gloss about her to face the dining-room and the meal that followed. Her clothes were good and with her newly acquired skills at make-up she felt as secure as she was going to feel. A glance in one of the mirrors assured her that she didn't look anything like a scared mouse and she straightened her back and assumed a cool look that should please Guy. It looked aristocratic, countess-like, her delicate face composed.

It did not please Guy.

'If you are to sit like the icemaiden then there will be some doubt in the minds of the staff as to whether or not we are on honeymoon,' he observed caustically, glancing angrily at her composed face. Her composure fled at once.

'Do they know...? How do they know...? Surely you haven't...?'

'We have the honeymoon suite,' he informed her drily, his eyes disparaging. 'We are also getting a deal of tender care from the waiters, who are beginning to look at you with less admiration and more concern. No doubt they are beginning to conclude that we have already enjoyed our wedding night and that now the whole thing is a bore.'

Lucy's face flushed painfully, her eyes looking down at her plate, his sudden hard laugh making her jump.

'Do not worry. The waiters are filled with admiration. Italians like to look at young women. They are looking so steadfastly at you that one or two guests are being sadly neglected.'

She glanced round uneasily and turned back very quickly indeed when she realised he was telling the truth. It didn't amuse Guy.

'Let's go,' he ordered curtly. 'We have finished and they are merely daydreaming. You are married to me.'

The remark did nothing for her confidence and she walked out as stiff as a rod, well aware that he was in one of his angry moods again.

'You would like to stroll in the gardens? It is not late and quite warm.' His voice sounded infinitely bored but Lucy wasn't at all bothered by that.

'Oh, yes, please!' She was almost feverishly glad, grasping the chance to keep away from their suite like a lifeline and he glanced down at her sardonically as they stepped outside.

'Finally, however, it *will* be late,' he pointed out and Lucy felt goosebumps shiver over her skin even in the soft night air.

There was a high bright moon like a lamp lighting up the night sky, its brightness fading out the brilliance of the stars, and Guy looked up, his dark face still and strange in the moonlight.

'Have you ever considered that it is the same moon which looks down on each one of us?' he mused. 'It is strange is it not that we think of this moon as shining for us alone when in fact it shines now in France, too, and in England. It shines on my château, on the glitter of Paris, even on your field of buttercups.'

'How do you know there were buttercups?' Lucy glanced at him curiously and a tight smile edged his lips.

'I have figured it out for myself, mostly, though it is imagination. I thought about your peculiar freedom as a child and imagined you running barefoot and alone through the fields; naturally they were filled with buttercups, the dream looked better that way.' He suddenly smiled down at her, his black mood gone, and she found herself smiling back.

'Imagination and dreams are not exactly the same,' she reminded him with solemn wisdom, and his grin widened.

'Are they not? You must tell me about it. Obviously my education is lacking.' He was still smiling as he took her arm, leading her out of the hotel grounds along the still warm streets, letting her gaze in shop windows and wander across the small piazzas, pointing out the great bulk of Etna against the moonlit sky. It was romantic, the soft breeze sensuous, stroking her skin, and Lucy relaxed without even knowing it, never flinching when he took her hand and held it firmly, his fingers entwining with hers. It felt like a romantic holiday and she had never really had a holiday before, romantic or otherwise.

The moon was no help at all, however, as they went back to the hotel, and in the lift all her tension returned. This was the night. She couldn't believe she had allowed herself to be manoeuvred into this situation. She turned impulsively to Guy, to beg him to reconsider, but his face stopped her. It seemed to have been carved from rock. He was standing tall and straight, looking at the closed doors of the lift, and her heart sank. He hated this too. He was remembering that it should have been Michelle. No wonder he distrusted women if he loved Michelle so much and she had married someone else. He had been gentle out there but now he was facing the inevitable. If she angered him it would only be that much worse.

The closing of the outer door of the suite sounded like doom and Lucy stood perfectly still, unable to take even one step towards the bedroom.

'You may shower first,' Guy said coldly. 'I will wait in the sitting-room. I will read.'

Her retreat seemed more like flight, she knew, but there was nothing she could do about it, and she leaned against the closed door of the bedroom hardly able to breathe, her eyes steadfastly refusing to see the huge bed, the turned-down sheets. Thoughts of escape came back into her mind, thoughts of getting out of the window and climbing down the thick creepers that covered the walls, but she was in a worse situation than she had been in before, even further from England. Her financial assets were still zero. Guy would catch her and be furious because other people would find out too. They would be right back here.

She went to shower and then fled to the bedroom again, standing looking out of the window at the moon and the lights that glittered on the sea as Guy came in quietly and as quietly collected his robe.

When he came back in, she turned to face him, her body stiff, her face white. She was too frightened to be thrilled by the sight of him in a short black robe, his hair still glistening from the shower, and he looked at her steadily before flicking off the lights, leaving her in the softer light of the moon.

The silver light flooded over her, turning her pale face into a translucent glow, her eyes large and dark, widening

as he came closer. Moonlight glinted on her arms and
through the thin gown she wore, her body seemingly
clothed in gossamer as he slid her robe away.

'Guy, *please!*' She managed a whispered plea as fear
curled along her spine but he didn't seem to even hear
her; his eyes were intent on her body, his hands on her
shoulders as he looked down at her.

'You may not feel like a bride, Lucinda, but you certainly look like one.' His voice was harsh, his face
curiously set, and he managed to make her feel that she
was an intruder, an intruder into his dreams about
Michelle. He even resented how she looked.

'We could forget all about it and nobody would know,'
she whispered through trembling lips.

'I would know!' His voice grated coldly and before
she knew what he was about he had swung her up into
his arms.

'Guy! *Please!*'

Tears came flooding into her eyes as he laid her on
the bed and for a second he looked down at her and
then he joined her, keeping his robe on and pulling the
sheets over them both.

'I am not a villain, Lucinda. I do not attack frightened
little girls. Go to sleep.'

The tears spilled over on to her cheeks, rolling down
with no hope of stopping and she didn't know whether
it was relief or fear or disappointment. Even so she had
to reply, her voice choked with misery.

'I—I'm not a *little girl!*' she sobbed. 'I know I don't
know anything and that I'm not Michelle but I'm not a
little girl.'

'No, you are not Michelle!' he rasped, his eyes burning
her even in the dim light. 'As to being a little girl, *Dieu!*
I do not know what you are!'

Her hand came up shakily to wipe at her wet cheeks
and his face suddenly softened.

'Don't cry, *ma belle*. In the morning things will not look so bad. Go to sleep with that thought. You are a countess now, eh? I do not think that countesses cry, at least I have never seen it and I have known several.'

'Did—did you make love to them?' Lucy asked foolishly, a sob in her voice and instead of anger she received laughter, soft and amused.

'If I had done, do you imagine I would tell you?' he mocked. His arm came round her and he drew her trembling to his shoulder. 'Stop your wild assumptions, *petite*, and go to sleep.'

She was grateful to snuggle against him, her mind anxiously asking her why she felt safe. A soft tiredness seemed to be invading all her limbs and she yawned sleepily.

'You'll never have an heir,' she commiserated, and he laughed again, a sound as dark and soft as the night.

'I am resigned to it,' he murmured drily. 'At least I have a countess. Perhaps I will leave all my estates to you when I die.'

'It's wicked to say things like that,' Lucy chided, her face against his chest. 'It's tempting fate. You're sure to be punished.'

'I have already been punished, *ma chére*,' he muttered ironically, and she knew he was thinking of Michelle. It made her unhappy and she gave a little whimper of protest, a small sound that was lost in the silence of the moonlit room. He heard it, apparently, because his hand came to her face, tracing her tear-wet cheeks, lingering there when she made no move to cringe away.

His warmth began to ease her fears and the sleepy lethargy faded as he caressed her cheeks, his hand wandering to her slender neck and smooth shoulders and Lucy gave in to the temptation to move even closer, her body softening against his warmth.

Guy turned towards her, his arms tightening her gently to him, and she lifted her face to look at him, as the moonlight softened the hard planes of his cheeks.

'You see a monster?' he asked softly, and she shook her head, her eyes wide and dark in the moonlight.

'You are almost fragile,' he murmured, his eyes roaming over her delicate, entranced face. 'Even so, I do not think I will fatten you up after all. I seem to prefer a slender flower in my arms.'

It reminded her that she was in his arms, tightly in his arms now and her face flushed as she realised that she wanted to be there.

'Guy.' She suddenly wanted to tell him that she wasn't afraid any more but his finger came to her lips.

'Ssh,' he whispered. 'I will just hold you. There is nothing to fear.' He held her for a second but his hands seemed to gain a mind of their own, moulding her shoulders, stroking her neck beneath her hair and shivers of pleasure shuddered over her skin at the skilled persuasion of his fingertips.

'Ssh.' He stroked her hair and tilted her face to his and when his lips closed over hers she submitted gladly, her mouth trembling open as he deepened the kiss until she had no thought in her mind but to stay there forever.

'Lucy!' Without even knowing it her head had gone back to allow his lips to caress her throat, his kisses burning against her skin and her little groan was not fear at all. 'Lucy!' he repeated thickly as his hands came to cup her breasts and his mouth closed over hers again.

She wanted to beg him to let her go but her body was treacherous, refusing to move away, refusing to fight, and she knew she was welcoming him, urging him on. Guy's hands found their way beneath her gown, easing it away until her skin was drenched in moonlight.

'The moon is lucky to see so many things,' he murmured thickly. 'Now it sees you—as I see you.' His eyes roamed over her, an almost hypnotic look in them, black and burning. 'No one has ever touched you, have they? This is your fright, your terror of the unknown. Perhaps you were meant only for me, mine to take and enjoy.'

It reminded her that she was afraid but her small moan of protest was lost beneath his lips.

'No, Lucy,' he muttered hoarsely. 'You are my wife and you will marry me—tonight!'

Fear came racing back but his hand swept along her thigh, stroking heavily over her stomach and cupping her breast and another wave of feeling shattered the fear before it had even begun to take effect. Pleasure flamed through her limbs and her lips parted in wonder, softened and vulnerable as he claimed them possessively.

Her tormented body moulded itself to him and he groaned deeply, his head moving down until his tongue found her breast in a rough caress that sent shafts of pleasure and pain through her. His tongue played carelessly with her, moving from one swollen breast to the other until torture grew inside her and she gave a cry of bewilderment and frustration.

'Come here.' His voice was deep and husky, not like Guy's voice at all, and her mouth fused with his as he moved completely over her, making her realise that the short black robe was gone as their skin met and burned. She clung to him as his mouth crushed hers, all thoughts of escape completely gone. Her only desire was to ease the aching pain inside and only being close to Guy could do that. Passion carried them along and her body arched closer as his strong hands lifted her and subtly parted her thighs.

Her arms were tightly around his neck, her body willingly pliant, but at the first thrust of his possession fire raged through her, forcing a scream to the surface, a scream that was cut off by his mouth as he held her rigid body tightly. It wasn't like any imprisonment though, it was comfort and a strange understanding. How could Guy know how she felt? He was a man.

The warmth of his arms brought relaxation slowly and tears found their way to her cheeks as he remained perfectly still.

'I—I'm sorry,' she whispered, her voice choking. 'I've never... You're my first...'

'Do not be sorry, *petite*,' he whispered back, his voice dark and soft. 'I was perhaps too eager to own you. Forgive me. You are my first wife, after all.'

It was funny, tender and it made her smile, her eyes meeting his as he looked down at her in the moonlight. But subtle feelings shivered to life inside her and as she softened Guy's smile died, his eyes beginning to burn into hers until Lucy's eyes closed languidly, her breath a gasp in her throat as he began to move inside her, reawakening all the burning pleasure.

She could feel his urgency mounting, his breathing harsh and uneven and sensation lifted her on fluttering wings as she threw back her head and called his name fervently. He captured her, crushing her mouth, his hands feverish on her.

'Now, Lucy!' he muttered harshly. 'Now you are my wife!'

He seemed to be inside her mind as well as her body, forcing her into unendurable rapture, his power over her without limit. She soared into the moonlight on wings of molten gold, hanging there for timeless throbbing minutes, brilliant lights all around her, all thoughts vanquished in this glimpse of heaven. And then she was hurtling back to earth with Guy's hard arms around her, tears streaming down her face as she pressed it against his heated skin.

'I'm sorry. I'm sorry.' Lucy was repeating it over and over without any real thought and Guy moved, drawing her to his shoulder, his breathing still unsteady.

'Sorry that you are crying, or sorry that it had to happen at all?' he queried huskily. 'Crying is not unusual after the most shattering experience of your life.' He drew her closer still, his hand stroking through her hair. 'Go to sleep, Lucinda.'

He had called her Lucy while he was making love to her. Had he forgotten in the heat of the moment or was it just to please her at the time? She turned away but his arms tightened, holding her to him.

'Go to sleep with me, not alone,' he ordered, suddenly harsh.

She turned her face against his shoulder, her body still shuddering with feeling and the hard arms wrapped her close, his face moving against her hair. She could feel emotions in him that were not contentment. Now that the moment had passed he was remembering who she was and who she was not.

'Guy? Are you——? Are you—sorry?'

Her whispered question didn't seem to surprise him but it was a while before he answered; in fact she thought he was not about to answer at all.

'Sorry?' he repeated, his voice darkly intense. 'Sorry that this had to be? Yes, I am sorry. I am sorry that I had to trap you, sorry that your first lover will not also be your last, sorry that a few moments of magic will not be a silver thread that weaves itself through your days. No doubt you are more sorry than I.'

He moved impatiently and drew her more tightly to him.

'Go to sleep!' he ordered coldly. 'You are an oddity. No other woman has turned to me and asked me if I was sorry.'

'You haven't had to make love to anyone else out of sheer necessity,' Lucy pointed out mournfully. If he could see into her heart he would be as shattered as she was.

She loved him and she knew that was a complication he could well do without.

'Perhaps you do not know what necessity is?' he rasped. 'Go to sleep and let me do the same or necessity may once again enter my mind.'

Colour flooded her face in the moonlight and she was thankful he couldn't see. She made a surreptitious movement to free herself but his hand tightened on her waist, his arm around her like a band of iron.

'A wife sleeps in her husband's arms,' he murmured implacably. 'That is two things you have learned tonight.'

Three, Lucy thought, sleepily tremulous. Three. I learned why things are dull when you're not there. I learned why I feel warm with you. I learned that I love you. Tears threatened to come back when she thought of the final days of this 'marriage', of her parting from Guy, never to see him again, but she choked them back. It was something he would never know, something he must never find out. His plan for the future did not include a wife, not a real wife.

When Lucy woke up Guy was already dressed. He was standing by the mirror, fastening his tie, and for a moment she was able to simply watch him, to almost gloat about the way he looked. The white shirt was stretched across broad shoulders, the grey trousers hugging lean hips. His hair was catching the sunlight that came streaming into the room and she lay looking at him unguardedly, her face colouring when she suddenly realised that he knew perfectly well that she was awake; he was also watching her, through the mirror.

'Good morning.' He turned and looked at her for a second and then walked slowly towards her, looking down at her as she lay with the sheet tucked up to her chin. 'How do you feel?'

'Perfectly fine.'

'In spite of everything,' he finished for her a trifle sardonically. 'You feel up to breakfast downstairs or do I send for some here?'

'I'll go down with you if—if you'll just let me...'

'Have a bit of privacy? I intend to find a morning paper. It has suddenly occurred to me that in seeking a wife I have been neglecting my financial interests. I had better see if I can get a French newspaper.'

'Shouldn't you be in Paris? I mean...'

'Probably. However, I am here.'

'We could go back now,' Lucy pointed out, blushing when the implications of her remark were obviously not lost on him. For a moment he regarded her steadily, an almost wary look in his eyes, and then his lips quirked.

'Having paid for a honeymoon, I intend to have one. After breakfast we will see the place properly and arrange what we are to do with our day.'

'You're talking as if this was a holiday,' Lucy pointed out a little crossly, alarmed at the way her heart began racing each time he looked at her.

'It is.' He watched her flushed face intently, seeing the blue of her eyes darken and then lighten again as emotions swept through her. His eyes narrowed and for a second he looked extremely cautious but the smile when it came was mocking. 'It is a holiday that is supposed to be very sweet, a *lune de miel* no less.'

'Under normal circumstances,' Lucy said sharply, hurt by the taunt.

'You did not find last night sweet?' He leaned over the bed, his hands on either side of her, trapping her so that all she could do was look up into his dark face. 'I found it sweet. It grows sweeter upon reflection.'

His eyes moved over her lips slowly, like a caress, and her heart bounded in her chest as she realised he was thinking about kissing her.

He straightened up instead, his dark eyes intent on her bewildered face.

'When you are dressed, I will meet you in the dining-room,' he stated coolly, the guarded look back in his eyes. 'Do not be too long. I am hungry.'

He just walked out, and Lucy got out of bed and went to shower. He was definitely on guard, not about to let her get close. After all, why should he? It was all over now. The only reason they were staying here was so that nobody back at the château would suspect that this was not the real thing.

She was filled with depression when she went down to breakfast, and Guy was little better. He had his paper and he looked so grim that she wondered if the whole of the market had crashed during his absence. The waiters watched them glumly and murmured to each other. Poor things, their romantic thoughts were no doubt taking a beating.

She enjoyed the day after all because, after a bad beginning, Guy's mood lifted and they talked easily to each other as they moved like the tourists they were through the town. She was fascinated by everything, much to Guy's amusement; the only thing she declined to do was take a trip up Mount Etna to see the bubbling lava, her rather fierce refusal adding to Guy's already amused expression.

This time she wasn't afraid of the night. She had wondered on and off throughout the day what would happen tonight. Would Guy sleep in the sitting-room of the suite? Would the arrangement be awkward? She was so sure he would have planned something that she was entirely at her ease, crushing the longing to be held in his arms again.

Of course there was only one bathroom and she showered and washed her hair first, sitting at the dressing-table and wielding her drier when Guy col-

lected his robe and disappeared into the bathroom later.
She was so intent on her thoughts that she didn't hear
him come out and the first thing she knew of his presence
was when her drier was taken from her fingers as Guy
switched it off.

'I'm not ready!' she began but he swung her round
towards him.

'I am!' he muttered thickly, sweeping her up into his
arms and making for the bed.

'Guy! It—it's not necessary now!' She was shy and
excited all at the same time, wanting to be back in the
sweet violence of last night, wanting to be lost in him.
All that Guy seemed to feel was determination.

'How do you know it is not necessary?' he murmured, dropping her in the middle of the bed and coming
down with her at once. His eyes moved over her face as
she gazed at him helplessly. 'We do not know if you are
already carrying my child.' He stared at her punishingly,
his eyes darkening further. 'In any case,' he added in a
voice that was almost bitter, 'there are various kinds of
necessity and my own is uppermost in my mind at this
moment.'

They stared at each other for a second, Lucy's face
white at the harsh sound of his voice although her body
was already sending messages to her that she could not
ignore. He watched her closely and then with a low groan
gathered her against him, tilting her mouth for the hot
kisses he poured on her. Their lips clung together and
as her body softened and melted into his he lifted his
head, looking into her eyes.

'I once suggested that you had a talent for this and
now I know that you have,' he murmured huskily. 'Your
gift is to melt into a man's arms, to turn into sweet honey,
to be soft and willing. You need no other gift, Lucy.'

He was calling her Lucy again although she had been
Lucinda all the day and his voice was soft and low,

thrilling her. She smiled into his eyes but he did not smile back. Instead he caught her even closer, his eyes holding her until the smile died from her lips.

'Look at me,' he ordered thickly. 'Look at me as I hold you and remember who it is who is taking your sweetness, your innocence.'

She didn't need to look at him. He would be burned into her mind and body forever, his face was almost part of her soul.

She had no time to speak even if words would have come because Guy was holding her against the power of his body, murmuring in his own language, caressing her urgently, and she gave herself up gladly, her body moving with his, enveloping him in sweetness, every bit of love in her pouring out towards him.

This time she felt that it was Guy who was shattered. He gasped her name in an agonised voice as they left the world together and later he lay against her, his face between her breasts, his lips continually planting small kisses against her skin.

'Is this what you learned in the meadow of buttercups?' he asked huskily after a while. 'Did you walk barefoot to the river, dreaming up ways to ensnare a man? I cannot move from you. You are an enchantress.'

Lucy laughed softly, her hand stroking his dark head. 'I'm not much at all,' she pointed out quietly, but his head rose and he looked up at her.

'You are not glamorous,' he agreed slowly. 'You are peculiar in your own small way.' His hands moved experimentally over her, his lips smiling. 'There is also not very much of you but what there is seems to have bewitched me.'

She stifled the small hope that leapt inside her. He was a sophisticated man. He would naturally say things like that to a woman. It was necessary to make sure he had an heir and he was making it as easy as he could for her. The smile died out of her eyes and she turned her head away but instantly he was over her, alert and intent.

'What is wrong, *petite*? I have said something to alarm you?'

He turned her face to his, looking deeply into her eyes, and she avoided his gaze, anxious now that he had not left her, wanting to retreat into herself.

'No. You've not alarmed me. I'm grateful to you for making this as easy as possible. I know that you don't like it any more than I do and...'

He swore under his breath, jerking her up until she was arched below him, her body a slender bow.

'*Dieu!* You are an oddity!' he grated. 'Last night you asked me if I was sorry. Tonight you thank me for my consideration. What if I were to tell you that I do not feel considerate, that I want you like this?'

He crushed her beneath him, his lips ravaging hers until she felt desire shudder through him, a desire he was not at any pains to conceal. It was nothing that filled her with fear. At least he wanted her, even if this was all a pretence. Her body softened against him and instantly the black passion fled as he stroked her closer.

'You know far more than you imagine,' he murmured against her lips. 'Not many women can change my mood with one sigh.' She felt tears fill her eyes at the thought of other women but he breathed his desire against her skin, his intent whispers sending shivers of delight through her, and he possessed her almost tenderly and later she fell asleep curled against him, his arm strangely protective, his deep breathing assuring her that he too slept with some sort of contentment.

In many ways it was a week of happiness although she could not say that she knew Guy any better. She knew his lovemaking, knew his strange moods that ranged from black anger and total silence to amused gentleness, but the man himself was still a complete mystery to her. He was warily aloof the moment she made any move to be closer. The only closeness he would allow was when he made love to her and even then he seemed to resent it that she could make him feel anything at all. Passion raged inside him whenever he held her close but his mind remained his own and Lucy dared not intrude.

As they stood in the suite and waited for their luggage to be collected on the last day, Lucy felt mournful. In spite of her determination to show no feeling her legs seemed to lead her to the white bedroom with the view of the sea.

'You are saying goodbye?' Guy came and stood beside her as she gazed out of the window and she kept her head carefully turned away.

'I don't suppose I'll see anything as beautiful again,' she said truthfully. If Guy was not there she would see no beauty at all.

'Of course you will, you strange creature,' he said, and laughed. 'The world is full of beautiful places and you will visit plenty of them. In any case, you will be able to come back here.'

Without Guy? Her heart cried out in denial but her tongue protected her.

'When I'm a rich ex-countess with pots of money I've earned, you mean?' she enquired coldly.

His reaction was furious and instant. He spun her round, glaring down at her. 'The shrew has returned, I see!' he bit out. 'I thought we had vanquished both the mouse and the shrew. Obviously we are not yet in control of them!' He crushed her against him, his mouth grinding into hers, ignoring her muffled cries until he suddenly relaxed and began to kiss her gently. He was holding her so close that she could feel every muscle in his chest, his legs hard against hers, and she groaned although the pain had stopped. They were simply clinging to each other, Guy's lips moving over hers passionately.

'You are too kissable,' he muttered, his eyes intent on her pale face as he lifted his head. 'Did I hurt you?'

'No.' She looked at him stubbornly, her only defence. He had hurt her but it was not the harsh kiss that had suddenly softened. It hurt to think that one day not even a harsh kiss would come to her from Guy.

'Then there is no harm done,' he snapped caustically. 'Let's go.'

It seemed to set the tone for the future, because the Guy who had held her in his arms and called her an enchantress simply ceased to exist when they returned to Paris and the château. His recently neglected financial affairs took him away constantly and Lucy was left alone for most of the time, coping with her new lifestyle as best she could.

Often he was overseas for days on end and he never asked her to go with him. Why should he? she asked herself. This was a marriage of convenience, made for only one reason. The time now was one of waiting and Guy needed her no more. No doubt there were other women. He was too virile, too experienced to be without female company even if Michelle was out of his reach.

Her loneliness and unhappiness were all the greater because she could not confide in anyone. In any case, there was nobody to tell. She only wanted to tell Guy and even when he was there she knew she could not mention anything.

If she became pregnant her world would be darker still. She dreamed of having Guy's baby, wanted it desperately, but she would be expected to go, to leave it behind. Could he be so cruel? Could he make her go, never see her own child again?

Yes, he could. He would simply remind her of the bargain or look at her as if she were odd. He often did that. He was in very little but when he was she would find his eyes on her as if he was making quite sure she was mentally stable and capable of bearing a child to continue his line. She prayed it would never happen, that he would tire of waiting and send her away where at least she would not have to see him and want him.

Finally the thing she had been subconsciously dreading happened. Guy came home one day to announce that there would be a dinner in a couple of days. She took the news in silence, a thing that seemed to readily bring on his black moods.

'Where will it be?' she asked after he had glared at her and said absolutely nothing.

'As I am giving it, it will be here,' he snapped, turning away in annoyance as if the sight of her irritated him utterly. 'You will have the chance to be hostess. It is a thing long overdue.'

'I—I can't!' The words were out before she could stop them and in any case she knew her own shortcomings well. This place was like a palace; she wouldn't even know how to begin and Madame Gatien terrified her because the woman had not softened one bit in all the time she had been here. She daily brought things to Lucy's attention that Lucy had no thoughts about at all and when Véronique was there the woman turned to Véronique and ignored Lucy totally. To begin to plan a dinner party with Madame Gatien was like having a lovely day with Count Dracula.

'What do you mean, you can't?' Guy rasped, swinging to face her. 'You are my wife, the Comtesse de Chauvrais. Can't is a word that is not in your vocabulary!'

'I know my own vocabulary,' Lucy snapped, angered by his refusal to accept any weakness at all. 'The word can't figures largely in it and I can't plan a dinner party for your friends and associates!'

'Véronique will help you,' he bit out at her, beginning to turn away again, his impatience obvious.

'Véronique is in Cannes and you know it!'

'Then Madame Gatien will help you,' he muttered, tired of what was to him a clearly stupid discussion.

'Into the jaws of death! Thanks a damned bundle!' Lucy raged.

'*Dieu!* You will not speak in that coarse way!' His eyes blazed down at her and she blazed right back.

'I can't help it, it's my lowly upbringing; artists, poets, thieves . . .'

He grabbed her and hauled her tightly against him, fury on his face, but she stood her ground. She had been hurt by the way he had ignored her, even though she knew why, but this was above and beyond the call of duty as far as she was concerned and she wasn't going to do it.

For a long second they glared at each other and then his eyes began to laugh as his long lips quirked in amusement.

'I remember saying that your peculiar ways would amuse me endlessly,' he began, but Lucy did not let him finish—she was too hurt.

'Not endlessly,' she pointed out bitterly. 'Only until the baby can be left and then I'll be running fast and far. After that you can get yourself another paid clown.'

He went very pale and she was sure she had gone too far but he let her go so suddenly that she almost fell. He did not notice. He turned away abruptly.

'Until then, countess, you carry the responsibility for which I will also pay,' he grated. 'There will be a dinner. If it is a shambles you will still face it at my side. Get your help wherever you think fit but the date is set and the guests will arrive. You will greet them standing by me and if you wish to be barefoot and in rags you will

still be there. You will be there when we dine, as befits
your position.'

'And what exactly is my position?' Lucy asked bitterly.

'You know that as well as I do,' he reminded her with
equal bitterness. 'You will have my child and then run
as far and as fast as possible. I am amazed you have
forgotten; not two minutes ago you pointed it out to
me.'

CHAPTER NINE

LUCY didn't get the chance to approach Madame Gatien. Guy had gone again and as soon as she was alone the rather forbidding face of the housekeeper appeared. She had her notebook at the ready and Lucy knew without doubt that Guy had informed her about the dinner party, making sure that Lucy could not carry out her threats.

'You would like to discuss the dinner party, *madame*?' The icy cold face gave nothing away and Lucy took her courage firmly in both hands and faced her for the very first time.

'I would like to discuss it, Madame Gatien, but it will do very little good. I'm not at all used to this sort of life as you've no doubt realised. Arranging a dinner party is quite beyond me.'

'The countess will perhaps take the responsibility?'

She meant Véronique and Lucy felt her face flush. This woman had ignored her ever since she had been here.

'She is in Cannes, *madame*, and will not be back in time. I will take the responsibility and I'll help but you will have to help me too. I know absolutely nothing about arranging dinner parties and certainly not on the scale that the count expects.'

Madame Gatien looked a little nonplussed for the first time ever. 'If I were to—to assist in your arrangements, *madame*, the servants would perhaps...'

'Think less of me?' Lucy asked candidly. 'I'll have to risk that, Madame Gatien. It's better to face their

154

surprise than face the count's annoyance when things go
wrong, surely?'

It was a trump card and Lucy realised that in all prob-
ability there were few in the château who had not at
some time faced the count's wrath, especially now when
he was so clearly bitter and angry, waiting for this time
to pass so that he could get on with his life.

'Very well, *madame*. We can perhaps keep things to
ourselves?'

Lucy smiled and motioned to a seat. 'Thank you. Sit
down and let's get on with it now.'

It clearly was not going to be the beginning of a
beautiful friendship but Lucy saw no reason to pretend
to be somebody she was not and Madame Gatien must
have organised hundreds of functions for Guy. If
Véronique had been in command then no doubt the
housekeeper would remember and pull things together.

She did. It took quite a long time but when she left
she looked rather satisfied with herself and Lucy
breathed a little easier. It had made a nice change to
have someone to talk to. If Guy neglected her much more
and if Véronique went to her own apartment in Paris
when she came back then Lucy felt she would soon forget
how to speak at all.

Guy did not return and as the day of the dinner party
drew near Lucy knew without much need of second sight
that he was deliberately staying away until the event so
that he would not have to see her. She would have felt
angry under normal circumstances but circumstances
were anything but normal and she had a very listless
feeling that seemed to be growing daily.

The florist's van came and Lucy was at great pains to
avoid seeing the man. She went to her room, a suite of
rooms that she and Guy occupied, each with a separate
bedroom because Guy no longer slept with her when he
was home. She was there when Madame Gatien came in

some time later, the usually icy face flushed with
annoyance and what looked a great deal like panic.

'Is something wrong? Surely the dinner party
is——?' Lucy began but Madame Gatien merely looked
more agitated.

'Everything is going well, *madame*. The chef is delighted with the menu and things are well under way. It
is the flowers. The arrangements for the tables have not
arrived and the man says they were not put on the van.
It is too late now to——'

'I'll do it.' Lucy got up immediately and walked to
the door but the housekeeper just stared at her anxiously.

'It is for a very important dinner party, *madame*.
Normally the flowers——'

'Well, things aren't normal, are they?' Lucy pointed
out. 'The gardens are full of flowers, in fact I can't
understand why we don't do our own.'

Later, as she foraged in the kitchen for suitable containers, the staff came to a virtual halt as they watched
her slim, jeans-clad figure busily occupied. It was the
very first time she had ever ventured into there and they
took it rather well as Madame Gatien explained the crisis.

'It looks beautiful, *madame*!'

Lucy and the housekeeper stood back to survey the
table later—much later, because it had taken over three
hours to select the flowers and arrange them. They
looked very good though, Lucy had to admit. It was
something she had always liked doing but she had never
had so many beautiful blooms to go at before.

'I'd better get changed.' Lucy glanced at her watch
and realised how short a time there was before the guests
would arrive. She was horrified to see that her hands
and arms were cut with picking the roses, some of her
nails broken, and Guy's mention of a farm servant came
back.

'Oh, *madame*! Your beautiful hands!'

Lucy hurried away, startled that she had beautiful hands. Maybe Madame Gatien thought she needed some sort of boost to her courage. She thought that too.

Guy came at the last minute, showered in his own bathroom and then walked into the sitting-room they shared. She wasn't ready and he tapped on her door.

'Lucinda? They will be here almost immediately. Surely you can be ready when you have had nothing to do all day but bathe and dress?'

Grumpy as usual, Lucy thought with a grimace. She kept her thoughts to herself and called that she would not be long, hearing him walk away angrily.

She looked at herself and sighed. She felt lethargic, the burst of energy that had appeared as she did the flowers now gone. The cream satin of her dress showed the faint gold of the tan she was beginning to get, one that had started in Sicily, but under it she looked pale, her eyes once again over-large in her face. Her hands were still scarred with rose thorns and there had been little she could do about it. They were beginning to sting too but her nails looked all right. She took one last anxious look at herself and went down to join Guy.

It was all a great success. Most of the men were businessmen with their wives, one or two of whom were particularly nice to Lucy, whether from choice or because they had been told to act well she did not know. No doubt their husbands were anxious to keep on the right side of Guy. He radiated power and Lucy had no doubt that he would use it as he thought fit.

Albert Colliot was there but not Michelle and he spent a great deal of time talking quietly to Guy, who frowned and nodded but whose eyes strayed frequently to Lucy as she sat looking a little fragile at the other end of the huge table. The frowns were for her. She was fairly sure

of that and after dinner when they all went into the white
and gold salon for coffee and drinks she found out why.

'What have you been doing to your hands?' he rasped
in a low voice, drawing her to his side. 'It is small wonder
you were not ready if you have been digging holes in the
garden. I am greatly surprised that there is no earth
beneath your fingernails!'

She couldn't answer. She had felt tearful and tired for
days and now she had to stand there and take it from
Guy with no chance to turn on him. Not that she wanted
to; she was weary of all this, weary of being lonely and
unloved by the man she wanted more than anything in
the world. She pulled away and walked to the other end
of the room, choking back tears, and Guy's eyes followed her, threatening and angry.

It was a great relief when they all went, Albert Colliot
hanging on until the last minute to talk to Guy again,
and Madame Gatien appeared as the last guest departed.

'It was a great success, *madame*,' Guy said to her with
one of his tight smiles. 'The choice of food was excellent
and the table was spectacular, the flowers astonishingly
beautiful. Surely it is not the same florist?'

'No, *monsieur*. The countess and I planned the menu
together but I am afraid the florist let us down, not for
the first time. The countess did the flowers herself, a
long and very skilled task.'

'My stepmother? I did not know she had returned.'

'She has not, *monsieur*. The *countess* did the flowers,
Comtesse Lucinda. She has a great flair for such things,
the staff are much impressed. We were in a panic but
she saved us. Did you notice, *monsieur*, that the small
containers were soufflé bowls? It was impossible to tell,
no?'

She gave what must have been a very rare smile because Guy's eyebrows shot up and he turned to a very
flushed Lucy.

'*You* did them?'

'Somebody had to,' Lucy muttered, wishing that Madame Gatien would go away and not stand there smugly with her hands folded in front of her like a prison guard.

'The *countess* pointed out, *monsieur*, that as we have huge gardens and several gardeners it seemed to be rather wasteful to have flowers delivered from Paris to arrive sometimes jaded and sometimes not at all. Two of the maids would like to learn how to do them if the countess would teach. The larger arrangements she would probably like to do herself; they are not easy as you can see from the centre piece on the table. That alone took an hour and complements the silver ideally.'

'We will discuss it,' Guy said, still looking shocked. 'Goodnight, *madame.*'

She almost bowed away and Lucy made for the stairs. She did not want Guy telling her that she should remember she was his wife and not some kitchen maid or florist. When he called to her she ignored him and ran quickly up to her room, closing the door and beginning to pull at the zip of her dress, tears blurring her eyes.

Guy was not easily dismissed. He simply walked in and spun her round as she refused to face him.

'I have hurt you.' He didn't miss the tears.

'You haven't. I'm quite used to being snapped at. Hurt me as much as you like.'

'*Dieu!* Don't say that!' He pulled her into his arms, tilting her face to his when she struggled, holding her still and looking at her tear-filled eyes. 'Poor little Lucy. I snarled at you because of your hands and all the time the cuts were there because you had to rescue the event from other people's inefficiency.'

'You didn't know. You just assumed, as usual,' Lucy said bitterly. 'How would you know that things go wrong? You're never here.'

'It is because I——' He stopped abruptly and then pulled her close, burying his face in her hair. 'There are many things you do not know, Lucinda, so many things.'

'You mean I'm ignorant?' she snapped, desperate that he should not see how much she needed to be held close.

'I mean no such thing,' he countered sharply, his dark head raised as he looked down at her. His face suddenly softened as he saw her hands on his chest, limply holding him off. 'Your beautiful hands. They are scratched and torn. If you are to take over the flower arrangements, then you must have gloves. You want to do it?'

'Yes.' She looked up at him breathlessly. She had expected him to order her to keep out of domestic arrangements. 'I love doing it and I could teach the maids. We could have the gardeners grow flowers especially for the house.'

'They did, in my mother's days,' he said, suddenly sombre. He brightened almost at once, though. 'They will be pleased, and clearly your skills will be talked of for some time. You appear to have captured the heart of Madame Gatien, your cobra.'

He was laughing down at her and Lucy blushed brightly.

'That was unkind. I shouldn't have said it.'

'You are never unkind,' he murmured. 'You have a sharp little tongue but it is only used for self-defence. I have noticed that.'

He looked down into her face and she felt waves of feeling begin to cloud her mind as his eyes stayed on her soft trembling mouth.

'Why do I find you so kissable?' he muttered, almost to himself, as his lips closed over her own.

She felt the zip of her dress propelled downwards, the cool air on her skin, and he ignored her murmured protests as he slid the dress away and lifted her into his arms.

'There's no need now,' she began, tears streaming down her cheeks. 'We're back to normal, not on honeymoon. I'm just working for you now, Guy!'

'Shut up!' His face tightened, paling almost to match her own and he crushed her against him, carrying her to the bed, his face against her hair. 'I don't need an excuse to make love to you. I am your husband and you are my wife!' He put her down and leaned over her before joining her, a deep groan leaving his throat as his arms wrapped around her, his body over hers. 'I want you, Lucinda,' he confessed huskily. 'Bewitch me again. Enchant me!'

She was incapable of resisting him and his gasp of pleasure as she moved against him told her one thing at least. He might not love her, he might still love Michelle, but he wanted her fiercely and this time there was no drawing back. He did not leave her room all night, his hunger for her insatiable until she fell into a deep dark sleep, her skin burning from his kisses, her body sweetly pained.

Next morning he was gone and Lucy lay still, looking at the sunlight as it streamed in at the windows. She felt strange, unreal, as if she were floating. It was an effort to get out of bed and then an even greater effort as she had to make for the bathroom very fast indeed, nausea gripping her blindingly. She stared at herself later in the long mirror as she leaned against the cool tiles.

She was pregnant. Deep inside she had known it for some time but now she was sure. Her feelings ranged between joy and misery. She was having Guy's child and she knew she could not bear to think of any other woman carrying his children. It would soon be over though. She would look after it until it was old enough to be handed to a nurse and then she would never see Guy again. The thought gave her such a pain that she held her hand to her stomach, sickness rocking her all over again. She couldn't face it! She would steal the baby, beg to be allowed to stay! She sobbed bitterly, making herself feel worse.

Madame Gatien knocked and came in as she was just coming back into her bedroom and Lucy was stunned to see that she had a tray, breakfast arranged on it. It was the first time ever that anyone had brought breakfast to her in her room and she had never imagined that the occasion would bring Madame Gatien herself.

'You are ill, *madame*?' She stopped as she was about to walk to the door, her eyes on Lucy's pale face. She seemed quite concerned and Lucy managed a smile of sorts.

'I'm all right, thank you. I'll be right down when I've eaten.'

Madame Gatien nodded but she looked thoughtful and left rather slowly as Lucy got on with her breakfast. She could have done without it. She still felt sick and she was determined to keep it from Guy as long as she could. Perhaps she would be able to escape and he would never know, never be able to take the baby from her. Then she would have part of him forever. She shook her head blindly. It was all so much fantasy. This child she held inside her was the future Comte de Chauvrais. She had no right to deprive it of this inheritance.

She wondered where Guy was now. Her face flushed as she thought of last night and shafts of pain seemed to slide right through her. He had not seemed to be able to get enough of her. She had never thought he would be like this. The cold-blooded marriage she had expected had not come to pass. If only he loved her. It was only when she was in his arms that he was in any way normal.

Even last night had started with a quarrel because he chose to think the worst of her. All the same, she wanted to see him, to hear his voice.

'Do you know where the count is?' she asked shyly, as she saw the housekeeper when she went downstairs.

'He went out, *madame*. I believe he had a call from Madame Colliot.'

It took all the joy out of Lucy's face. Michelle! So he was seeing her. Then how could he make love as he had done last night? How could he whisper that she entranced him, that he could not stop kissing her? Her mind went blank with misery, her heart heavy.

She went out into the garden, a gentle smile on her face as she encountered André, the son of one of the gardeners. André was small, dark and inquisitive, a little boy of seven, and he had taken to following Lucy around like a happy puppy. He talked endlessly in his mixture of French and peculiar English and Lucy listened with amused interest as he talked about his father very proudly, about his school and his holidays. Every time she moved, he followed her until her sadness left her and she settled down beside him on the grass.

She was there when Guy came and she looked up as she saw him coming across the grass. His face was set and unsmiling and André sprang up, brushing down his clothes quickly, giving a comical little bow.

'*Monsieur le Comte,*' he said with amusing gravity.

'André.' Guy returned the bow gravely, his sombre eyes suddenly smiling. 'I am happy to see you.'

'*Merci.* I am caring for your lady.' The little face was a study of propriety and Lucy was fascinated by the small scene.

'You have my thanks. I will take her indoors,' Guy said seriously and André nodded his understanding, walking off with the extraordinary dignity of a child. Lucy looked at Guy and he was grinning widely.

He glanced down at her, the smile touching her astonished face.

'It never occurred to me that you even knew of his existence,' she said.

'We have a long-time understanding,' Guy murmured, taking her arm and walking her towards the house. 'His dignity is newly acquired. Not too long ago he was a small monster and broke at least one window each month.' He grinned. 'We reached an agreement. He is now my spy, reporting any mischief to me. Beware, my lady, you are under his scrutiny.'

'I see. And I thought it was my charm.' Lucy smiled, cherishing this small moment, her love for Guy threatening to make her legs weak.

'We are having guests tonight,' he announced as they went into the small salon. 'The Colliots are coming. It will be a small, informal dinner party, nothing to worry you. I have business to discuss with Albert and we can use my study.'

'I'm to entertain Michelle Colliot?' Lucy asked tightly, suddenly remembering where he had been today. Was this meeting to discuss the situation? Was Albert Colliot prepared to divorce his wife?

'For a while,' Guy said, his smile dying as he heard her strained voice. 'She will not attack you.'

'Though she may think about it!' Lucy snapped bitterly. 'Will she help you to look after my child when I've gone?'

'He will be my child too!' Guy rasped.

'You haven't got a child yet!' Lucy's voice was brittle with misery if he could only have noticed but he was angry now, blazingly angry.

'I intend to make quite sure that I do have a child.' His smile was mockingly cruel and she flushed painfully.

'I realise that,' she admitted huskily. 'I'm not in any doubt as to why you make love to me.'

'Aren't you?' he snarled, pulling her tightly into his arms. 'Do you not think that I work at it rather industriously—all night, for example?'

Her cheeks flamed and her eyes looked wildly blue as she stared at him, wondering what he meant. It was only a second's embarrassment, though, because the whole world began to spin and fade and the last thing she heard was Guy's voice as she slipped quietly into a faint.

When she came round Guy was bending over her as she lay on the long settee and Madame Gatien was bustling in with brandy.

'She looked most unwell this morning, *monsieur*. If you had been here I would have told you then.'

'I know now,' Guy muttered, his hand cool on Lucy's hot face. 'Telephone the doctor and tell him it is an emergency.'

'No!' Lucy managed as the housekeeper turned to go. 'I don't need a doctor.'

'The telephone, Madame Gatien!' Guy snapped as she seemed to hesitate between orders and his tone assured her who was master still. She went.

'I don't need a doctor,' Lucy murmured quietly, turning her face away. 'I know perfectly well what's wrong with me. I'm pregnant.'

He was silent for so long that she began to wonder if he had heard at all.

'How long have you known?'

Guy's face was white as she turned to look at him, his eyes shuttered and still and she would have thought he didn't want a son at all if she hadn't known better. He just stood looking down at her as if she were telling him something dreadful.

'I've known for a while but only for sure today. I—I was sick. I felt odd, floating. I thought at first it was because...'

Her face flooded with soft colour at what she had been about to say. She had thought at first her strange feelings were because of the night with Guy, because of his fierce, insatiable lovemaking.

Colour touched his face too and he dropped on his knees beside her, pulling her into his arms gently.

'Oh, Lucy,' he muttered hoarsely. 'I thought you would be perfect for my plans but now I look at you and I see how fragile you really are, how young. Lucy, I——'

She never knew what he was going to say because Madame Gatien came back in, her eyes still anxious, and to Lucy's surprise she wasn't a bit put out to see Guy kneeling and holding her.

'The doctor is on his way, *monsieur*. He will be but minutes. Should I get the countess to her room?'

'*I* will get the countess to her room!' Guy snapped, scooping Lucy up and walking to the door. 'You will wait here for the doctor and show him up!'

All the doctor did was confirm what Lucy already knew and when he left, after strict instructions about her diet, Guy came back in, walking about with his hands deep in his pockets, saying nothing at all until Lucy felt like crying all over again.

'I will cancel tonight's dinner,' he said finally. 'You are not to tire yourself. I will expect you to rest frequently now.'

'There's no need to cancel the dinner,' Lucy told him gloomily, thinking that if he was planning to be with Michelle she would rather know now than later. 'Madame Gatien and I will manage perfectly well.'

'I do not wish you to be under any strain while you are carrying my son.'

It was all he cared about, the end of his great plan, and Lucy's lips tightened at this callous way of thinking.

'I can't promise a boy!' she said bitterly. 'What happens if it's a girl? Do you extend my contract or make new arrangements with someone else?'

The eyes he turned on her looked to be almost on fire and then he walked out of the door, saying nothing at all. When she got dressed and went downstairs he had gone again. What of it? She would finally say goodbye forever not only to Guy but to the baby she now carried inside her. She might as well get used to it, but she knew she never would. She loved Guy and soon she would love his child, although neither of them would really be hers. She went to find André. At least she had someone to talk to even if it was only a seven-year-old boy.

The dinner party was all she had imagined it would be. Guy and Albert Colliot were locked in serious discussion as soon as the meal ended and Michelle's eyes were sharp on Lucy's face. Finally Guy took Albert to his study and Lucy had to face Michelle alone, hating to even look at her, loneliness and jealousy making her more unhappy than she had ever been.

'You are managing well, I see.' Michelle leaned back, crossing her elegant legs and lighting a cigarette. 'It is not easy to be the Comtesse de Chauvrais. I gave up the idea.'

'I didn't realise you'd been offered the position,' Lucy murmured. It merely amused Michelle. She threw back her beautiful head and laughed.

'A quaint way of putting it. Surely Guy has not become so very courtly. I have known him for many years and he has always been a very sensuous man, one to sweep you off your feet, not offer you a position.'

Lucy kept her face very still. He had offered her a position, after all, forced her into it, and clearly Michelle knew his lovemaking.

'Anyway,' Michelle said, her hand sweeping round the grandeur of the room. 'I couldn't take all this. I'm very ordinary. I told Guy.'

As ordinary as a tarantula.

'He asked you to marry him?' Lucy asked carefully.

'Oh, don't be anxious, my dear,' Michelle soothed, the gleam of malice in her eyes. 'It was a long time ago, before you came on the scene. I've known Guy for years and he's never had any trouble getting what he wanted, even now my skin shivers at the thought of it. I couldn't take this place though and that stepmother——'

Lucy sprang up, pain searing through her at the thought of this woman in Guy's arms. She had to get out of here.

'Please excuse me,' she muttered. 'I feel sick.'

'My dear Lucinda! I hope I haven't upset you. Guy and I hardly meet now—well, not too often.'

'You haven't upset me,' Lucy flared. 'After all, he married me. I really do feel sick. You see, I'm pregnant.'

She fled from the room and at least she had the satisfaction of seeing Michelle's face go pale, seeing those glossy nails bite into the soft palms.

She *was* sick. The tension had been too much. She didn't go back down and Guy must have packed them off early. Even so, Lucy was in bed when he came into her room.

'Lucy? You are ill?'

He sounded desperately anxious and she turned her face away.

'I'm quite all right. The early months are supposed to be the worst.'

'I was in the study. Michelle did not tell me until we came out,' he said bitterly. At least it sounded bitter, ut then he would be feeling like that, being with Michelle's husband and not alone with her as he would no doubt have liked to be, as he had also no doubt been with her earlier this day.

'It doesn't matter. There was nothing you could have done.'

'No. It is all too late now.'

'It's exactly what you wanted, a small amount of my time. Eighteen months at the most, you said. How long has it been now? How long do I have to serve yet?'

'Don't! *Mon Dieu*, you can look like an angel and injure with your tongue at the same time!'

'Have I injured you, Guy?' she asked wearily. 'Surely I'm the one who's injured, captured, blackmailed, pregnant?'

'Lucy!' His voice sounded almost broken but she turned away, Michelle's poisonously beautiful face filling her mind.

'Please go away, Guy. I promise to rest, to take care. It's not an easy way to earn money and a title but I'm in it now for a while.'

Over the next few months she hardly saw Guy at all. Business took him away and she was not invited. When he had bought clothes for her he had said that she would need clothes to be with him but he seemed to have forgotten that. He phoned her from Rome, from Venice and even from Paris although it was merely a matter of a few miles away. Clearly he did not want to come home at all and the only consolation she had was the baby, its presence now quite obvious.

The staff spoiled her, Véronique seemed to haunt the place, but the one she wanted was never there. When he did come she was painfully shy, her condition no longer able to be disguised, and the look in his eyes embarassed her.

His gaze seemed to be unable to leave her face or bod and he stood away from her, his whole being held stiffly

'You are well?'

'Yes. I've got over the morning sickness. It was onl the first three months. I—I manage to get a lot of ex ercise and the doctor sees me every week. It's no necessary but he said that you—you...'

'Insisted? Yes, I did.'

'You needn't have,' Lucy assured him quietly, lookin away. 'I'll take care of myself. I have the baby to thin about. I know I have to be careful. You needn't worr that I'll do anything to jeopardise——'

'Perhaps I am more concerned about you than th baby,' he murmured intensely. 'I have been very worrie about you.'

'You're very strong-willed,' Lucy informed him in softly bitter voice. 'All that worry and yet you were abl to stay away and contain it. I admire you.'

He was by her side in two strides, his hand on he arm, holding it tightly. 'Lucy!'

She pulled away, upset at his nearness. If he had bee here all the time she wouldn't have minded but now h had come suddenly and she was so very pregnant, s ungainly.

'Let me go, Guy,' she whispered. 'You don't need t be near me. I'm not a very pretty sight and the plan i going well. There's no need any more to——'

'For pity's sake! If you were not like this I would shak the life out of you!' he raged. There was so muc suppressed violence in him, in his voice, in his taut body that Lucy went pale, her lips trembling. She felt ver vulnerable, utterly defenceless.

'Faint again and I will see to it that you stay in be for the rest of the time,' he threatened, his arms comin round her.

'I'm not going to faint. Perhaps you could manage not to shout so much? I've been reading that unborn babies can hear music. What do you imagine he's hearing now? You sound like Etna!' Her voice was stiff and she threw her head up proudly, meeting his gaze. She was holding herself like stone, afraid to let any part of her touch him, and his face softened as he glanced down at her.

'So you have decided that you are carrying my son after all?' he asked in a suddenly indulgent voice.

'Yes!' she informed him in as cold a voice as she could manage. 'The plan worked. It will all be over soon and I'll be on my way.'

His grip tightened, his face icing over and cold dark eyes stared into hers. 'Maybe I will want three more!' he rasped acidly. 'If I do, I will renew your contract!'

Surprisingly, he stayed close. He went to his office in Paris daily but the long absences seemed to be over. He might just as well have been away, though, because he never actually came close to her. He was more like a cool, polite stranger and she began to think that the times he had held her and whispered passionately to her were imagination. If she hadn't been carrying his child she would have been sure of the fact.

Véronique was there often and by this time she was fairly close to Lucy and Lucy was glad of her company. She had André to talk to too and he was improving her French. Madame Gatien watched over her severely but Guy was always in her thoughts.

She was crossing the hall one day as Guy was coming out of his study and his face was so stony as he saw her that she knew he couldn't bear to look at her. She hurried out of the house, never glancing back, tears blinding her eyes, and at first she didn't see André.

He was by the lake, throwing stones as far as his arm
would throw and she dried her eyes quickly before he
could turn and see her. Before she was near him he ben
to find more stones and in a sort of slow-motion terror
she saw his feet slip on the mud, his small body sliding
into the lake, the tall bulrushes hiding him almos
immediately.

'André!' She began to run, ignoring the stitch in her
side that came like a dagger. He was already out of her
sight and she plunged into the dark, cold water withou
any hesitation, grasping his sleeve and managing to lif
his head clear of the entangled weeds.

She was screaming for help, hanging on to hin
although he seemed to be so heavy with the water in his
clothes and suddenly, like a miracle, Guy was there
lifting André to the bank.

She could see Véronique and Madame Gatien running
too and Guy rapped out orders to them.

'Take him, Madame Gatien! He is cold and shocked
Véronique, get out my car quickly!'

He lifted Lucy out but she was stiff, cold, the stitch
in her side worse than ever and as her feet touched the
bank she swayed dizzily.

'Guy! I feel—feel ill. The baby!'

She felt Guy's arms sweep her up and then everything
was black, nothing left at all. She remembered the car
Véronique beside her. She remembered her own voice
calling to Guy telling him over and over that she was
sorry, that she couldn't help it. She remembered the
hospital corridors and Guy's face like marble, cold and
set, his lips edged with white. He never seemed to look
at her and his hand held hers as he walked beside the
trolley, his fingers hurting. She told him that but he did
not seem to hear.

CHAPTER TEN

LUCY was in a narrow, white bed, flat powerful lights in the ceiling. There seemed to be a lot of people there too, all of them busy but it was hazy, unreal.

'There is no miscarriage, *Monsieur le Comte*. The shock of her experience has brought on the birth but only by a week or so, it was almost due.'

She could see the doctor, his rather round face reassuring, but Guy was out of her range of vision, only his deep voice assuring her that he was there at all.

'How is she?' His voice sounded harsh and Lucy felt a wave of dread. If she had lost his child, their child...

'Weakened somewhat and, as I say, shocked. She is less fragile than she looks, however, and there are great resources of strength in a woman at this time that as a mere man never fails to astonish me.'

'I want—I would like to stay.'

'When everything is ready we will bring you back in. For now, though——'

Pain tore through Lucy, bringing a cry from her lips that she could not stop and instantly a cool hand was on her wrist, a sympathetic face leaning over her.

'Doctor!' the nurse called, but Lucy's cry had already brought action and Guy came too, his face so drawn that for a second Lucy just stared at him. Pain came again in a blinding rush and sweat broke out on her face, her hand reaching out instinctively to the nurse for help.

It was Guy's strong hand that grasped hers, his dark eyes filled with shock.

'I am staying!' The words seemed to be forced through stiff lips and the doctor shrugged.

'Perhaps you had better. We seem to have arrived at the crucial time a little more quickly than I anticipated. You will need a gown and mask.'

She needed him to be there but his presence filled her with anguish. This was the end, or nearly so. She was bearing this pain for Guy, for his son, for a child she would be forced to leave. Between bouts of savage pain she looked at Guy as he watched her intently, only his eyes visible above the mask. He was afraid, she could see it. Would his son have the same eyes, dark and deep? Would he have Guy's dark hair, his superb strength? Some of those things she would never know.

Tears came into her eyes and Guy wiped them away.

'Lucy!' His voice was husky, almost trembling, his grip on her hand tight.

'I'll manage it, Guy. You'll have your son,' she moaned, her voice rising as more pain slashed through her.

'Use the pain!' The doctor's voice was almost over her head. 'It has a purpose. Use it! Push!' His voice became exasperated. 'You will have to leave, *monsieur*. She cannot seem to concentrate with you here.'

'She needs me!' Guy's voice was taut, anguish in it, but the doctor was adamant.

'It is difficult for her, the first child, her shock. Sometimes, *monsieur*, at times like these a woman even hates her husband for a little while, the pain is great but do not worry, she will love you again when the baby arrives.'

Behind the mask Guy's face was white, his eyes stark as he looked at Lucy, but she was too involved to see anything, an almost animal cry of pain leaving her lips, and Guy was persuaded outside as the doctor came back to her.

'Now, *ma chère*! Let us get down to some hard work,' he announced grimly.

It was a boy, beautiful, perfect, and Lucy lay exhausted as he was placed in her arms.

'We have done it, *madame*,' the doctor announced, as he grinned down at her cheerfully, his mask hanging around his neck. '*Mon Dieu!* I am worn out.' His eyes looked sympathetic as his smile softened. 'It was not easy, I know. Your first child, the shock. It will not be like that next time, I promise.'

There would be no 'next time', Lucy thought, her eyes on Guy's son. The time would be quick now, the days soon over, and she would never see either of them again. She could not even cry now; her emotions were drained, the prize after such pain not hers at all.

Guy came a little later but while the doctor was still there, his eyes on Lucy even as the door was opened for him.

'A little time only, *monsieur*,' the doctor said as he left. 'She is exhausted. It was a difficult birth.'

She heard the words but it didn't really register in her mind and she was still gazing entranced at her son when Guy sat beside her.

'Lucy?' His voice sounded hoarse and she glanced up.

'It's all right. He's perfect. He's exactly like you.'

'With blue eyes and a bright red face?' Guy's smile was strained as he looked at the small being in Lucy's arms and his hand came out to touch him tentatively, his finger tracing the velvet skin.

'His face is red because he had to work very hard to come into the world,' Lucy said quietly. She looked almost solemnly at Guy. 'What are you going to call him?'

'I thought we would name him together.' Guy sounded uncertain, hesitant, and she supposed he didn't want to hurt her, to remind her that this was almost the end, and that she would have to leave the baby behind when she had fought so hard to get him.

'Gerard,' she said quietly, looking away as he stared at her in surprise. 'I know it was your father's name. Véronique told me.'

'What about your own father's name if we are to name him after fathers?'

'Eric?' She looked away again. 'My father was English.'

'So is our son, partly so.'

'Only for now,' Lucy whispered, her eyes closing. 'He's going to be a French count. He probably won't even know he has English blood.' It was hurting so much to talk normally when she wanted Guy to take her in his arms, to tell her she had given him a beautiful baby, to tell her he loved her.

'Lucy!' His voice sounded ragged, as if something tore at him, but she kept her eyes closed in case she pleaded with him to love her, to let her stay forever.

'I'm very tired, Guy,' was all she said.

'What about this, *madame*?' Madame Gatien came in leading two smiling maids who were carrying a rocking-chair. 'I knew it was somewhere in the house, in some unused room.' She beamed on Lucy and Lucy's face lit up with pleasure.

'Oh, Madame Gatien! It's just perfect! How did you know I wanted one?'

'I have seen you rocking the baby back and forth as you fed him. It is instinctive, good for both mother and child. I have three children of my own, now, of course grown up,' she explained, marshalling the two interested maids to the door of Lucy's room and closing it firmly behind them. 'I used to rock them too.'

It was hard to believe how the housekeeper had changed, Lucy thought. She was her constant champion, looking almost ready to intervene on Lucy's behalf if Guy was at all morose.

He was almost constantly moody now and hardly ever at home. Sometimes she thought he regretted the whole thing and didn't want the baby and that hurt almost as much as the knowledge that he didn't want her either.

She moved to the rocker that had been cleaned and polished with loving care in the kitchens and Madame Gatien used the excuse to hurry to the small room next door that was now a nursery, coming back with Guy's son in her arms.

'Four months, *madame*. How the time has flown. He will soon need a nurse so that you can take your place beside the count when he travels.'

Lucy smiled wanly but said nothing. Yes, he would soon need a nurse and then he would not need her at all, and neither would Guy. She smiled down at the baby as Madame Gatien left very reluctantly. Gerard Eric. Guy had insisted, and for some reason he also insisted upon calling him Eric even though Lucy complained that it didn't suit him one bit.

On the odd occasion that he had come in when she was feeding the baby he had rapidly left as if the sight of the baby at her breast embarrassed him. Perhaps it reminded him she was still necessary, still had to be here?

Lucy sighed and began to feed the baby, who reacted hungrily, nuzzling against her contentedly. It was her only consolation and that for very little longer; tears filled her eyes. How could she leave him? She began to rock gently and the small eyes closed dreamily.

She did not hear the door open and it was only a slight sound that alerted her to the fact that she was not alone. Guy stood watching her; there was a faint flare of colour on his cheekbones, and his lips were tightened.

'I didn't know you were here,' Lucy said quietly. 'I'm afraid I can't stop, it's feeding time. If it embarrasses you perhaps you could come back later?'

'I need an appointment?' His eyes swept over her, lingering on her breasts. 'It does not embarrass me,' he said in a strange, husky voice. 'Perhaps, being but a man, it would do, but you make it seem so natural.'

'It is natural,' Lucy said solemnly. 'It's good for both of us.'

'So I am informed.' Guy ran his hand along the back of his neck as if he was tired and she noticed how strained he looked, how strained he had looked for ages, come to think of it.

'Are you having any trouble?' she asked softly. 'Any business trouble, I mean?'

He walked over to the window and looked down at the gardens, glad apparently to be able to have his back to them. His laugh was hard.

'I am glad you decided to clarify that. No, I am not having any business problems.' He swung round. 'I have been talking to the doctor. He believes it would be good if you could continue to feed the baby yourself, as long as you can. What do you think of it? I know that originally I said it would be for only a little time but——'

'Thank you. I'd like that,' Lucy said quietly, her eyes determinedly on her son, the chair never faltering in the steady rocking. He had been asking the doctor how long it would be necessary for her to stay, perhaps not in so many words but clearly he wanted to know.

'What do you mean, thank you?' Guy asked explosively. 'You are——'

'Odd, peculiar? I know,' Lucy managed quietly, her quiet voice seeming to infuriate him more because he strode across, towering over her.

'*Ciel!* Will you stop that rocking and look at me!'

She made no move to obey and he rasped her name, his voice threatening.

'Lucy!'

'You forgot to call me Lucinda,' she pointed out softly. 'You even say Lucy now when you're angry, which is most of the time. I can't really understand why you're angry, Guy. Everything is exactly as you planned, just as you wanted it.'

'Is it?' She didn't look up and he came down on one knee in front of her, his hands grasping the chair, stopping the even movement, and she looked up then, expecting rage. In fact she had been trying to make him angry, anything rather than the moody, polite way he had all the time now. He was so distant from her, as if there had never been any time when he was near.

He wasn't glaring at her though, his eyes were on her breast, his face flushed and his eyes darkened.

'Will you stay?' he asked without looking up.

'I'll stay as long as he needs me.' She had no doubt at all about what he meant. The doctor had probably given him a lecture on the benefits of breast-feeding.

'It may be a long time,' he murmured, his eyes still on her breast and the small being who sucked hungrily. 'You are perhaps afraid that if you go I will call him a small monster and act accordingly?'

He meant *when* she went not if. Her hand stroked the small head so close to her.

'How could you? He's beautiful.'

'Yes. He is.' His hand captured hers, raising it to his lips, and she looked down at the two dark heads so close to her, response searing through her body. Loving him was a sweet agony, an endless torture.

He bent his head and his lips brushed her breast close to the baby's head, his hand sliding into her blouse to curl around her other breast and caress it.

'Guy!' Pleasure shot through her like a pain. It was almost barbaric, erotic, but his lips followed his hand, his tongue stroking across her skin.

'Don't stop me!' he muttered thickly. 'I am sick with wanting you.' His hands grasped her waist and the baby murmured, his senses alert to the change in Lucy. It seemed to bring Guy to his senses too and he stood, moving away, his flushed face now pale.

'I'm sorry, Lucy. Forgive me,' he said hoarsely. 'Sometimes I cannot seem to help myself. Deep inside you there must be a witch.'

She wished there were. She would put a spell on him and never leave. Her body was shuddering with feeling, bitter-sweet pain, and she rocked back and forth, tears in her eyes, trying to be calm for the baby's sake.

When she was near she sometimes bewitched him, that was what he had meant, but it never brought him to her willingly and when she was gone he would forget. She looked into the clear blue eyes of her son, seeing his face through a blur of tears. He would forget too, Guy would see to that. It would not be convenient to have a child constantly asking for his mother.

In the afternoon, Véronique arrived. She was a regular visitor, delighted with the baby, and they settled down to tea when the baby finally slept.

'He is beautiful and so like Guy,' Véronique said with a contented sigh. 'I sometimes wondered if he would ever marry, if the name would die out with him. His distrust of women began at an age when he was utterly vulnerable to them. I suppose he has told you?'

'No. I haven't pried into——'

'You are not prying, my dear Lucy. I would have thought that Guy would have told you. He was sixteen when Gerard and I married and he was worldly even then. His mother was living with another man long before I came on the scene. She had already told Gerard that she was leaving him for good and that he was welcome to his son. She went to America with her lover and they are there still. We decided not to tell Guy, to even allow him to think that we were already having an affair, anything but that his mother could so callously reject him. He knew the truth, though. One day, darkly and quietly in a way that is so much Guy, he simply looked at us and said, "I know." He had heard their final quarrel, her words of rejection.' She leaned back with a sigh. 'I used to wonder if he still thought about her and I suppose he must have—his mother. For me it made things more comfortable. He accepted me, but Guy seemed to develop a distrust of women. I never cease to thank God that you came to him, Lucy.'

Lucy looked away quickly. Véronique was going to know eventually. Would she think that Lucy was leaving willingly? Guy's feelings were clearer to her now. At sixteen he would have been very vulnerable, just becoming a man and wary of women in any case. No wonder he didn't want a real wife. And Michelle had rejected him, only content to be his mistress. It didn't make things better but at least she understood.

Long after Véronique had left she sat in the darkening room but Guy did not come in. She went to bed with tears on her face, tears for Guy, for the baby and for herself.

She was feeding the baby the next morning when Madame Gatien brought her breakfast, a self-imposed task that she seemed to delight in. She informed Lucy that Guy was still at home.

'He was preparing to leave when he had a visitor; it is Madame Colliot. She looks distressed.' The housekeeper went out, not knowing what a bombshell she had exploded for Lucy.

Guy had probably told Michelle that Lucy was to stay for longer. When she left they would get together at last. Could that be what Guy was discussing so seriously with Albert Colliot at the dinner party? She knew by now that some people were divorced quite amicably, even still remaining friends.

She put the baby down when he had finished but she dared not go downstairs. To meet Michelle face to face would be too much. She walked to the window and looked down, drawing back in alarm as Guy came out to the steps with Michelle. She was still talking agitatedly although Lucy could not hear from this height. Guy was soothing her and finally he put his arm around her, hugging her close and kissing her cheek. It was all Lucy needed to see. Her face was like alabaster as she caught a glimpse of herself in the mirror but she knew what she had to do.

The doctor came in the afternoon, his visit quite usual. Guy seemed to think that something disastrous would happen if the doctor did not call daily now and Lucy was expecting him. Guy had not been up to see her. He left for Paris as Michelle did, his car behind hers, and Lucy was glad. She wanted all this settled before he came back.

'When can I stop feeding the baby?' she asked as soon as the doctor was seated.

'Whenever you like. I suppose you want to get out more with your husband? Many young wives do. The milk will stop if he is not feeding and I can give you tablets to help if necessary.'

'If—if I stop, will it harm him?' Lucy wanted to know, her face anxious, and the doctor laughed, his eyes on the chubby baby in her arms.

'Not at all. I doubt if anything will harm this little chap with the care that is lavished on him and the count's insistence on a daily visit from me. If either of you ever have a cold I expect to be called out of bed at least five times in the night.'

'So I can stop whenever I like?' Lucy asked, ignoring the way he added her to Guy's anxiety over the baby. He nodded cheerfully and she had all the information she wanted.

She didn't expect Guy to come and find her. Since the other day he had avoided her all over again but, as she was summoning up her courage to seek him out that evening, he came into her room after a brief knock.

'This afternoon in Paris I interviewed several women for the position of nurse to Eric,' he began without preamble and Lucy knew she had been right. He was desperate to have this thing over and done with.

'Did you find one that suited you?' she asked carefully, managing to force herself to look at him and keep some semblance of calm.

'Suited me? You will be the one to finally choose. I would not know how to begin. I only attempted to reduce the candidates somewhat.'

'You'll be dealing with her, Guy, whoever she is,' Lucy pointed out quietly. 'If you can't get on with her then she's not going to last very long and it would be bad for the baby to have a succession of nurses.'

'Why should I be the one to deal with a nurse?' he asked, his face tight and grim. His eyes roamed over her face as if he were looking for some secret there and she turned abruptly away, pacing about, because she was too agitated to stand still.

'When the doctor came today he told me I could stop feeding the baby as soon as I wanted. I can stop right now if necessary but I think he should be introduced to a bottle gradually. Maybe next week I'll be able to—to stop. I'll go then, of course, and you'll obviously have to deal with the nurse yourself. If I can sometimes see him...'

He was like someone carved from stone as he walked to the window and stared out at the gathering dusk. His shoulders were tight, his hands on either side of the frame, as he leaned his head against the cool glass as if he needed something to keep him steady.

'Only the other day you said you wanted to stay, to continue to look after him,' he reminded her harshly. 'Now you will be content to "sometimes see him". What has happened to make you change your mind?'

'Nothing I—I've just been thinking about it. It's best to go before the baby really gets to know me, it's better for him, that's all.'

'That's all?' He swung to face her, his eyes flat and dead in his face. His skin looked grey and drawn. 'You think he does not know you when he has nestled in your arms, suckled at your breast? You lay a hand on him and his crying stops. His eyes follow you as you move.'

'The longer I stay the more they'll follow me, the more he'll know!' Lucy cried, a sob choked back. What did he think this was doing to her? She was facing all this for Guy as she had faced everything for him.

'You care nothing for him, then? You can leave him without a backward glance? You can take your money and go just like any other employee and "sometimes see him"?'

'Stop it!' Lucy wept, her hands clenched together at her sides. 'What choice do I have? Do I stay until leaving him kills me or go now while I've still got the courage? I'll go now. You can think what you like. I might have known it would end as it began with you trying to trap me.'

'It should never have begun,' Guy said bitterly, 'but it will never end for me. Leaving him will kill you? You are killing me daily! I am dying with looking for love that is not there.'

'It will be there when I've gone.' Lucy looked at him with tears streaming down her face. 'You'll be able to go to Michelle with a clear conscience. I don't know what arrangements you've made, but——'

'Arrangements? With Michelle?' He strode over to her, jerking her against him, his hand hard against her face. 'What has she got to do with this? She has troubles of her own. Albert Colliot is on the brink of ruin and I am trying to salvage what I can of his affairs. Am I supposed to laugh in her face and send her on her way when she comes to me and begs for further aid for the man she loves?'

Lucy stared at him with huge, tear-filled eyes, unable to understand anything. What was he saying? Did he want her to go when there was no chance of Michelle coming to him?

'She loves him? But—but you—you love her! When I've gone——'

'I do not love her! I have never loved her! I know what you have thought and it has been my only defence against you. I had the chance to marry Michelle a long time ago and I had no desire to do so. She is spoiled, selfish and impossible, only now realising that she loves Colliot when he is on the brink of disaster. She has never meant a thing to me. I have always kept her at arm's length!' He glared down at her. 'When you have gone I will follow you!' he grated, his hand tightening on her chin. 'When you have gone I will haunt you, I will be there every time you turn your head. I will fight the divorce! I will drag you back by your hair!'

'Guy!' She stood shaking in his arms as they closed round her, stunned by his possessive violence. 'You wanted me to go. You're backing out of it and——'

'I had backed out of it before we were even married.' He looked down at her bewildered face and then gathered her more closely, his arms desperate. 'I want you close to me, much closer than this.' He suddenly lowered his head, his face in her hair. 'Don't leave me, Lucy, my strange little Lucy,' he whispered brokenly. 'I cannot face a day if you go. I love you so very much. I know you love the baby. I also know I can make you want me. Let's begin like that; perhaps one day you will come to love me a little if I try very hard.'

'Oh, Guy! Guy!' She threw her arms around his neck, hardly able to believe it. Her eyes were shining brilliantly blue through the tears when he looked up at her. 'You won't have to try at all. I love you terribly. It was breaking my heart to leave but I thought you wanted it.'

'Lucy! *Chérie!* I have never wanted it since you climbed the wall and sprang on me like an agitated little mouse,' he said thickly, his arms crushing her against him. 'I did not know it was love then but I knew you were somehow a part of my life.'

He covered her face and neck with desperate kisses, his arms pressing her close. 'In Sicily, that first night, I regretted the marriage, I didn't want it to be like that any more. I would have told you the next day and begged to start all over again but you entranced me, you were sweet and alive in my arms and I could not resist you. By morning I dared not tell you in case you left me.'

'You've been away so much I thought you wanted it all over and done with,' Lucy whispered.

'I tried to stay away. I wanted you too much,' he said urgently against her lips. 'I have fought against my feelings for you, knowing you would leave me. When I asked you to marry me you devastated me with your honesty. You simply said that you did not like me and would not like to be near me. It took a great deal of courage to look straight back at you and say it did not matter because it mattered very much, even then.' He buried his face against the soft warmth of her neck. 'Oh, *chérie,*' he groaned, 'when you had the baby, I could not take the pain from you, could not help at all. The doctor said that some women hated their husbands for a while, I knew that you would hate me always because there was no loving to begin with.'

'Oh, there was, Guy! I loved you all the time. I loved you then but I wanted it to be real.'

'It was real! It is real!' he whispered thickly. 'Lucy! My love!'

His arms tightened to lift her and she was more than willing but the sharp cry from the other room had Guy lowering her back to the floor, his face rueful.

'Our son needs a feeding bottle and a nurse with all speed,' he asserted wryly. 'I am not very good at sharing and I cannot contemplate the time when I will be prepared to share you, not even with him.'

Lucy smiled up at him happily, gently extricating herself from his warm arms.

'You'll get used to it. With a couple more children around you'll never even notice.'

'I'll notice, *chérie*,' he promised, his eyes gleaming, 'but I do not mind if you wish to experiment.'

They were back in Sicily, back in the same room that Lucy had loved, and Guy's arms were around her but now she knew it was for always.

'I wanted to come back here,' she murmured.

'Without me?' Guy looked down at her face, his dark eyes roaming over her flushed cheeks.

'Never without you,' she whispered. 'Even when I was running away from you, I wanted you to fetch me back.'

'Which I did,' he reminded her wryly. 'When the van driver telephoned me I raced up to your room and found you gone.' His arms tightened. 'I was not sure that he had you safe. It might well have been some other English girl, some hitch-hiker. He merely said that he had picked up an English girl and he thought she belonged to me. I knew you did not belong to me but I knew that you had to. I could not have let you go.'

'I did belong to you,' Lucy whispered, her lips teasing his stubborn chin. 'When you came storming towards the van I was delighted.'

'Then why did you run away, my darling?'

'I wanted you to love me, I suppose. I was hurt.'

His arms closed tightly round her, his lips caressing her face. 'Oh, Lucy,' he groaned, 'if you had only known even then how much I loved you, so much unhappiness could have been prevented.'

'I know now, Guy,' she murmured against his demanding lips.

'I wonder how the new nurse is managing?' she mused later as Guy held her close, nibbling against her ear.

'Véronique is staying at the château,' he reminded her soothingly. 'Everything will be all right, my sweet. In any case,' he added with a grin, 'if the nurse is managing to evade Madame Gatien she will be doing very well. One false move and *madame* will devour her. It is comforting that a dragon guards Eric.'

'Why do you persist in calling him that?' Lucy asked in mild exasperation.

'Because I thought you would finally leave me,' he confessed, punctuating his words with kisses. 'I wanted to be reminded every minute that part of him was you. I could not in all fairness call him Lucy.'

She giggled as he pulled her against him, his lips trailing over her shoulders seductively.

'I didn't know you were an idiot, Guy,' she laughed, squealing as his teeth nipped her.

'I was not until you came along. You stole my mind, enchantress, and now you have stolen my soul.' He drew back when she was breathless from his heated kisses, his eyes adoring as he looked down at her. 'Once you said that you were without talent, in fact you repeated it frequently. You have tamed a dragon, given gladness to Véronique, brought joy to a rather grim household, but

most of all you have given me happiness I never dreamed
of. You have the gift of loving, *chérie*, and I love you
so deeply that I cannot ever think of anything else.'

He pulled her close, his passion flaring over her, and
she sank into the sweetness of his love, her heart flying
like a wild bird as he possessed her. She was loved, safe,
Guy her own forever and her lips were smiling as he
brought her back to earth in his strong arms.

'I'm not afraid of anything any more,' she said
dreamily as he smiled down at her. 'Tomorrow we can
take that trip up Mount Etna to see the lava.'

'*Pas question!* I paid for another honeymoon and I
intend to spend it right here.' His eyes slid over her
sensuously. 'This time around you will tell me you love
me all the time, you will never leave my side.'

'What if I don't like this contract?' Lucy asked, her
eyes sparkling.

'You are stuck with it, and with me,' he murmured
against her lips, 'but there are compensations. I will make
love to you all the time.'

'I'll stay,' Lucy promised, as his smiling lips covered
her own.

"GET AWAY FROM IT ALL" SWEEPSTAKES

HERE'S HOW THE SWEEPSTAKES WORKS

NO PURCHASE NECESSARY

o enter each drawing, complete the appropriate Official Entry Form or a 3" by
" index card by hand-printing your name, address and phone number and
ne trip destination that the entry is being submitted for (i.e., Caneel Bay,
Canyon Ranch or London and the English Countryside) and mailing it to: Get
Away From It All Sweepstakes, P.O. Box 1397, Buffalo, New York 14269-1397.

lo responsibility is assumed for lost, late or misdirected mail. Entries must be
ent separately with first class postage affixed, and be received by: 4/15/92
or the Caneel Bay Vacation Drawing, 5/15/92 for the Canyon Ranch Vacation
Drawing and 6/15/92 for the London and the English Countryside Vacation
Drawing. Sweepstakes is open to residents of the U.S. (except Puerto Rico)
nd Canada, 21 years of age or older as of 5/31/92.

or complete rules send a self-addressed, stamped (WA residents need not
ffix return postage) envelope to: Get Away From It All Sweepstakes, P.O. Box
892, Blair, NE 68009.

© 1992 HARLEQUIN ENTERPRISES LTD.   SWP-RLS

"GET AWAY FROM IT ALL" SWEEPSTAKES

HERE'S HOW THE SWEEPSTAKES WORKS

NO PURCHASE NECESSARY

o enter each drawing, complete the appropriate Official Entry Form or a 3" by
" index card by hand-printing your name, address and phone number and
ne trip destination that the entry is being submitted for (i.e., Caneel Bay,
Canyon Ranch or London and the English Countryside) and mailing it to: Get
Away From It All Sweepstakes, P.O. Box 1397, Buffalo, New York 14269-1397.

lo responsibility is assumed for lost, late or misdirected mail. Entries must be
ent separately with first class postage affixed, and be received by: 4/15/92
or the Caneel Bay Vacation Drawing, 5/15/92 for the Canyon Ranch Vacation
Drawing and 6/15/92 for the London and the English Countryside Vacation
Drawing. Sweepstakes is open to residents of the U.S. (except Puerto Rico)
nd Canada, 21 years of age or older as of 5/31/92.

or complete rules send a self-addressed, stamped (WA residents need not
ffix return postage) envelope to: Get Away From It All Sweepstakes, P.O. Box
892, Blair, NE 68009.

© 1992 HARLEQUIN ENTERPRISES LTD.   SWP-RLS

"GET AWAY FROM IT ALL"

Brand-new Subscribers-Only Sweepstakes

OFFICIAL ENTRY FORM

This entry must be received by: May 15, 1992
This month's winner will be notified by: May 31, 1992
Trip must be taken between: June 30, 1992—June 30, 1993

YES, I want to win the Canyon Ranch vacation for two. I understand the prize includes round-trip airfare and the two additional prizes revealed in the BONUS PRIZES insert.

Name _____

Address _____

City _____

State/Prov. _____ Zip/Postal Code _____

Daytime phone number _____
                                    (Area Code)

Return entries with invoice in envelope provided. Each book in this shipment has two entry coupons — and the more coupons you enter, the better your chances of winning!
© 1992 HARLEQUIN ENTERPRISES LTD.   2M-CPN

"GET AWAY FROM IT ALL"

Brand-new Subscribers-Only Sweepstakes

OFFICIAL ENTRY FORM

This entry must be received by: May 15, 1992
This month's winner will be notified by: May 31, 1992
Trip must be taken between: June 30, 1992—June 30, 1993

YES, I want to win the Canyon Ranch vacation for two. I understand the prize includes round-trip airfare and the two additional prizes revealed in the BONUS PRIZES insert.

Name _____

Address _____

City _____

State/Prov. _____ Zip/Postal Code _____

Daytime phone number _____
                                    (Area Code)

Return entries with invoice in envelope provided. Each book in this shipment has two entry coupons — and the more coupons you enter, the better your chances of winning!
© 1992 HARLEQUIN ENTERPRISES LTD.   2M-CPN